RESCUE DOG
MYSTERIES SERIES
VOLUME 1

MICHELE ANNE O'NEAIL

authorHOUSE

AuthorHouse™
1663 Liberty Drive
Bloomington, IN 47403
www.authorhouse.com
Phone: 833-262-8899

Published by AuthorHouse 08/20/2021

ISBN: 978-1-6655-2855-9 (sc)
ISBN: 978-1-6655-2854-2 (e)

THE KEY TO THE "V"

A Rescue Dog Mystery
By: Michele Anne O'Neail

CHAPTER ONE

Stained glass windows exploded like shattered rainbows as the wrecking ball struck. Diane wondered if nothing was sacred anymore. The gracious old church was coming down to make room for a condo development, as were the five Victorian row houses just a few blocks to the east. She closed her eyes to block out the sight but had to look up when brilliant flashing lights intruded behind her eyelashes and the sound of a dog barking in distress filled the streetcar.

The driver's voice came over the intercom, "Might be stopped for a while folks. Emergency up ahead."

Police cars, a fire truck and an ambulance blocked the road in front of a tired, semi-detached-house; its painted shutters peeling away to reveal seventy years of color choices faded by the elements. The house was distinctive for another reason though. The front window and glass door were covered in magazine and newspaper clippings from the 1960's and 70's showcasing a blues musician, then in his prime. The observant streetcar rider might see the life story of the home's elderly occupant, so proudly displayed, as a sad and desperate need for validation, but the long-haired man who lived there with his curly coated dog, waving to all who passed by, seemed content, not tragic.

Diane looked out of the smudged streetcar window and breathed in sharply before jumping to her feet and dashing to the front of the vehicle.

"I have to get off now, please!"

"Might as well. We won't be moving for a while. Guess the old guy finally bought it. I'm calling for a shuttle bus if you want to wait."

"I just need off. Thanks."

A young police officer holding a leashed dog was having a hard time as the "Labradoodle" pulled hard, trying to get away.

"Diane Daniels. Animal Services. May I take over?"

"Be my guest! This dog is nuts. The owner is deceased and we haven't made arrangements for this guy yet."

"Deceased!?"

"He was found dead in his kitchen. The dog was lying beside him. Didn't want to move." The officer said as he gladly handed over the leash and stepped aside.

"He just needs to say goodbye." Diane whispered as she knelt down and stroked the dog's unruly hair.

"Hey Powie. It's going to be okay. Let's go see your daddy."

She choked back tears as she approached the stretcher that held the covered body of the dog's companion for the last two years. The excited dog let out a mournful whine and then lay down submissively.

"I'll take care of you buddy. Don't worry." Diane patted the animal's head and slowly walked him away from where his rescuer lay covered by a grey wool blanket that had the ominous word "coroner" printed at the bottom edge.

Knees shaking, she stepped back with the dog and sat down on the side steps of the house. She thought back to a day two years earlier when she had been handling intake at the shelter. They were full to the rafters when an older man wearing a battered jean jacket and a crazy colorful scarf, had walked in and stated simply that he wanted to adopt a dog. She had estimated him to be a senior citizen who would most likely be ineligible due to his age, just as the intake team had burst through the door with a Labrador-Poodle cross they had retrieved from the home of a local "hoarder" who had died that afternoon.

She recognized the animal. He had been brought in for temporary shelter a couple of times and then released back to the woman who loved him dearly despite her inability to keep a proper home. As Diane pulled up the dog's file on her computer, the animal control officer had slipped into the back room and the dog had gone over to the man with the scarf and laid his head in his lap.

"Can I take this guy? He likes me. And he looks kind of rough like me." The man with the long grey hair said with a lyrical laugh.

Diane observed the pair. She knew the dog was nine years old and would have a hard time being adopted due to his age. He was fairly healthy and used to limited activity, but she wasn't supposed to make snap decisions. They were at capacity though and anything seemed better than the fate that would inevitably await this animal. She got up from the desk and asked the man to tell her a little about himself.

"I'm Jimmy Freeman. I live a few blocks away and I've always wanted a dog. This guy would be lucky to get me because; pregnant pause…" the man said while gesturing dramatically. " I'm famous! Played my guitar all over North America and even went to Europe. I actually met George Harrison once! I opened for all the best bands in the sixties."

"How do you support yourself now Mr. Freeman?"

"The government takes care of me quite nicely, thank you very much. I own my own house and I have pensions and some royalties coming in from my music, so I can afford his food and vet bills if that's what you're asking. By the way, what's his name?"

"Powder."

"As in gun, or the stuff you sprinkle on yourself?" the musical laugh filled the office once again.

Diane watched the man gently rub the dog's ears and look into his eyes.

"Powder, would you like to live with me? I get pizza with stinky anchovies every Friday night and I go to the park to feed the squirrels every day rain or shine."

The dog leaned in toward his new friend and then turned to look at the woman in charge of his fate as if he somehow knew this was his best chance.

"I really shouldn't do this, but I think you two were meant to be together. I'll authorize you taking him if you let me come to your home to check up on things tomorrow."

"That would be just fine! I'll have tea and cookies ready! I always have my tea at 2:00 in the afternoon. Would that work for you?"

Diane Daniels agreed to the plan and input the information to make Jimmy Freeman the official owner of the dog named "Powder". Strangely, she didn't have any misgivings as she put a collar and leash on the dog and let the pair exit the building. Sometimes rules had to be broken to save a life.

She didn't know she had just saved two.

CHAPTER TWO

As the fire truck pulled away, a stern looking police officer approached and asked if Diane would take the dog to Animal Control. She told him she would take care of things and asked him what had happened to Jimmy.

"You know the deceased?"

"Yes. He came into the shelter a couple of years back and walked out with this guy." She motioned to the dog now clinging to her side. "I kept in touch with him. We last visited about three weeks ago."

"A neighbor called it in. He was dead on the kitchen floor. A lot of blood. Probably got drunk and fell. A full investigation will be done."

Diane looked at the officer and saw his visible disdain for the elderly man and his messy but eclectic home. Seeing how easily her eccentric friend's life was being dismissed, she fumed.

"Jimmy walked two miles a day in every kind of weather. He's been sober for twenty years!"

The officer noted the anger in her eyes and said nothing before leaving to join the fire crew who were getting ready to exit the scene. She tried to hear what they were saying but with all of the commotion, it was impossible and she needed to get Powie away from the trauma. As she started to walk away, the officer who appeared to be moving toward the front door of the house, called to her.

"Miss? Can you come down to the station later? You might have information that would be useful."

Diane nodded her agreement and crossed the road to take the streetcar back home, knowing that an eleven-year-old dog taken to the pound would have little hope of ever leaving. What was one more pet when you already had four? "Powie" as Jimmy had called him, was familiar with her little family. There was Abbie, the three legged German Shepard, Albert, the

Bearded Collie, Katie, a thirteen-year-old deaf Maltese, and Sally the blind Tabby cat. They all had their stories and he would fit right in.

Later that afternoon, as rain poured from a dismal sky, Diane made her way into the police station that was set up in a historic building just east of the city center. The modern interior had successfully incorporated etched glass and metal finishes that allowed the splendor of the old brick and woodwork to shine through, somehow making the atmosphere a little less heavy. The same officer who had spoken to her about her elderly friend now greeted her with a much more pleasant demeanor.

"Thanks for coming down in this awful weather. It's Diane Daniels right? Is the dog okay?"

"He will be. I'm keeping him."

"I'm sorry I was a bit abrupt earlier. We see a lot of these old guys dead in their homes. It's usually booze and drugs. I apologize if I seemed insensitive. Just a hazard of the job."

The officer took Diane to a lounge and introduced himself as Scott Harris. He wrote down her personal details and offered her coffee in a glass mug, which she accepted, wrapping her fingers around its soothing warmth.

"Do you know if Mr. Freeman had any next of kin?"

"No. He told me he was an only child. He was seventy-five in March. His parents were long deceased and he had never married or had children of his own."

"Lonely life."

"I didn't think of him that way. He was really successful as a musician in the early seventies, but when a contract fell through and he had some bad breaks, he turned to drugs and alcohol and spent a few years as a hard–core addict. He later cleaned up his act and went on to play the bar circuit here in the city and all around the province."

"Do you know of anyone who might want him dead?"

"Are you saying he was murdered?!"

The coroner's report will tell us more, but there is evidence pointing to something other than an accident. After you told me he was sober, we took another look. We aren't ruling out anything yet."

Diane leaned back and sighed. "Jimmy was the sweetest old guy. When

I visited him at Christmas, he and Powie were dressed up as Santa and an Elf and they had gone all around the neighborhood giving out candy."

"What was with his life story taped to his front windows?"

"I guess he needed people to know he had had his fifteen minutes of fame. I never asked, but he did point out the photos one time I was there and told me he was really proud of what he had done. He played his guitar every day. Music was a huge part of who he was."

"We found the will but it was taken into evidence and there will be more on that later."

"Honestly, I don't know of anyone who would want to hurt Jimmy. But it's not the best area and he did worry about those break-ins that happened a few blocks from his street recently."

"The house should be cleared as a crime scene within a week and then I will call you to pick up the keys."

"Why me? If there was a will, isn't there an executor?"

"He left you everything."

"Excuse me?"

The officer handed over a large envelope and said that she should read the letter inside. He then excused himself and said he would be back in a few minutes. Diane stared at the envelope. She had known that Jimmy was fond of her but surely there was someone else in his life more deserving. She opened the package and carefully unfolded the paper inside.

Dear Diane,

Well, if you're reading this, then I've croaked. I hope it was fast. I hate those long drawn out endings. Please don't be sad for me. I had a great life! I actually met George Harrison once! Did I ever tell you that? And I got to play music for years. All my life really and it was a blast! I want you to take Powie. He loves you and you will do right by him. That day you let me take him, and I know you were breaking the rules, was the best day of my life. I never told you, but before Powie, I was getting tired. I was thinking about ending it all that day when the arthritis made it hard for me to play. But something made me go into that shelter and the rest is history! I was so lucky to have that silly, gentle dog in my life. He made me live again. I walked all over with him by my side and met so many new friends. He slept in the bed with me every night and any feelings of loneliness I had were just gone. Thank you. You made that happen and you were always there for me. I hope you let some lucky guy into your life. I was too old for you girl or I would've proposed the day I met you! Please know how special you are. So, whatever I have left is yours. Except for my guitar, just give that to Lucas. The house is worth a bit in this crazy market but it has a small mortgage on it. The furniture is crap, so throw it to the curb. Some of my clothes are pretty cool so you can donate them, or heck, get them stuffed and displayed in a museum! But keep the records. They will be worth a lot one day. If there is any money in the bank or the government pays out for my corpse, donate it to the shelter. I'd like to think I had something to do with rescuing the next old dog that gets brought in with little hope of a good life. Look around the place and don't mind the clutter. Powie knows where the treasure is, wink, wink.

Love, your dear friend, Jimmy Freeman.

She couldn't stop the tears. Jimmy was such a wonderful old soul and she was really going to miss him. She wiped her eyes as Scott Harris returned.

"The report just came back. Mr. Freeman died from an intentional strike to the left temple with a blunt object. When we found him, there was a beer bottle lying beside him and when you told me he was sober, it didn't make sense so we took another look. The bottle matches with the shape of the wound on the side of his head."

"So he didn't fall."

"No. It appears he was the victim of an attack."

"I need some air."

"Why don't you go home? It's a bit of a shock I'd guess. I'll be in touch tomorrow. We can talk more then."

Diane shook her head in agreement and walked back out into the rain. The officer observing her could tell she was shaking as she left.

"Put a tail on her."

The constable Scott Harris had spoken to nodded. "Is she a suspect sir?"

"The old guy takes a blow to the head and bleeds out on his kitchen floor. No forced entry. She comes along at just the right time and takes the smelly old dog home like it's all a plan. And the kicker is, he left her everything."

"He lived in that old house with the magazines on the windows right? Funny how an old shack like that would be worth almost a million these days. Is that the motive?"

Scott stood up and spoke sternly to the constable. "Get on it, Chris."

Diane was happy to see Powie curled up with the other dogs on the antique couch she had found on the street waiting for the garbage pick up. She had dragged it home, painted the wood a light cream color and had painstakingly reupholstered it in an indigo blue paisley fabric. It fit in well in the 'shabby chic' first floor unit she rented in an old fourplex just a block from the lake. It was a place where she had finally felt secure. The spacious rooms, often flooded with sunlight, held a happy feeling, and for the young woman who had grown up through the foster care system in Canada's largest city, this was where she truly felt at home. She had completed her degree in social work but had felt too close to the situations she was supposed to be objective about to be effective. Her love for animals and her ingrained bent towards social justice led her to her current position as an administrator at the large downtown animal shelter where she had met Powie and the man who had loved him.

At the age of thirty-two, she was able to live comfortably, but she had no savings to speak of and now she had to process the fact that she had been left an estate. This was hard to fathom. She had been on her own more or less since the age of eight when her single mother had died. Her father's identity had never been disclosed, there were no living relatives and she had never been adopted. She did keep in touch with one of her foster mothers who lived close by, but she admittedly had a hard time letting people in. She was working on it, and Jimmy Freeman had been a big part of her healing. Their talks had exposed the ever-present hurt they both carried from years of being alone in the world. She had told him about her ten years in the Child Services system and he had shared his tale of leaving an abusive home at sixteen and aside from a yearly Christmas card he sent to his parents, never looking back. During a leisurely stroll along the boardwalk that past summer, Jimmy had told her about his years in Nashville in the 70's and how he had sort of had a family there.

"I spent a lot of hours writing songs at the 'Chipped Mug Café'. I don't think the place was really called that but nobody knew it by any other name! The people who ran it liked musicians and they didn't care if you bought one coffee and stayed for three hours. Janet, the waitress, knew everybody's favorites by heart and she could read your mind as you walked through the door and get you eggs poached medium with a side of toast and marmalade before you even thought about it. I got sick that winter and was stuck in my motel room for two weeks. Halfway through the ordeal, there's a knock at my door and Janet's standing there with a bag of food and a whole apple pie. She said she missed me messing up the counter. We never dated. It wasn't like that. She was kind of like a sister. Then that spring I noticed she was losing weight. She wouldn't tell anybody what was wrong, but it was cancer. When she died I got a letter from a lawyer and she had arranged to buy me a guitar I told her I wanted if I could ever get the money together. She paid off a loan for another friend and she left money to the local high school for prom dresses for girls who couldn't afford them. She told me once her prom was the happiest day of her life and it was all down hill from there. She'd laugh when she told you that but you could tell she wished she'd had the package, you know. The boyfriend, the wedding, the family. My song "After the Dance…" is about her. I just wish she had lived long enough to hear me play it on that special guitar."

Jimmy had taken a long breath and then looking directly into Diane's eyes had said;

"Girl, sometimes your family is kind of mismatched. Just good souls you pick up along the way. The trick is not to dwell on it or worry because it's pointless to do that. My parents hated that I didn't want to be a plumber. They didn't think playing in a band was anything special, but Janet, she lit up like a bolt of lightening when I gave her one of my promo photos taken by a professional photographer. She said she was proud of me. Proud! That's family."

Powie got up off of the couch and walked over to Diane. He looked a little confused but she could tell he was adjusting quickly. He had one of those faces that would make him look like a puppy well into his geriatric years. She kissed the top of his head. The sun was shining brilliantly and she decided to take the dogs out for a walk. The street was quiet, as most people had not ventured out yet after the relentless rain. Powie splashed through a puddle and wagged his tail as he saw the park up ahead. Stopping when they got down by the three dawn redwood trees that were known as the 'dinosaurs' of the city park, Diane looked heavenward, and said "Don't worry Jimmy. He's going to be okay with us."

The police cruiser drove slowly down to the bottom of the street and parked on the corner. Not much to see. Just a pretty young woman walking three very mismatched dogs through the sticky wet sand.

CHAPTER THREE

Looking at the only color magazine photo displayed in Jimmy Freeman's front window, the evidence specialist from the police station excitedly said, "That's a 1959 Gibson Flying V! If the old guy still had it today it would be worth about half as much as his house."

"Probably sold it for a fix." Scott Harris flung back with his usual jaded tone.

"Don't you ever lighten up? I couldn't do what we do if I always saw the dark side. This is really interesting if you take a look. Jimmy Freeman played a lot of famous places. He must've been very talented."

"Take photos of the articles. Sweep for prints in the rest of the house and let's get out of here. I'm more worried about finding the creep who beat up that lady in the convenience store last night because she wouldn't give him a free pack of cigarettes, than wasting my time on revisiting some guitar player's glory days."

Back at his desk at the station, Scott opened the report he had requested be run on Diane Daniels. After a quick read, he knew she was thirty-two, had been a ward of the city from the age of eight when she was orphaned, spent ten months in a juvenile detention center at age fourteen after being caught shoplifting and following her release, had lived with foster parents until she entered university on a full scholarship at age eighteen. She graduated with an honors degree in Social Work but resigned from her job with Social Services after a period of stress leave. She had worked for about $50,000 a year for Animal Services for the past four years. No tickets or driver's license suspensions showed up. She was leasing a flat close to the lake by herself and had one credit card that was paid on time but was close to being maxed out.

He closed the file and picked up the phone.

"Get Diane Daniels in here for questioning tomorrow morning."

He knew she was guilty. What would a beautiful young woman want with an old relic like Freeman unless there was money in it? He'd seen it before. Chat them up, gain their trust and then get them to make a will that signs it all over. Poor old guy had been a sitting duck.

With four dogs sleeping in a heap on her feet, Diane picked up her phone and checked her voicemail. A message from the police station asked her to come in at 9:00 a.m. the next day. The only friend of Jimmy's she had ever met, Lucas, had left a tearful plea for her to call him if she had any idea of what would be done to honor the musician. She hadn't even thought of that yet. The body might not be released for another week and she had no thought as to what to do. Jimmy had told her if he died he just wanted anyone who cared to meet in the park, play music and feed the squirrels. He did have a Facebook page he accessed on a computer at his local library from time to time but it had never been a big priority for him. She looked at it and saw that a number of his friends had posted messages of condolence and expressed their sadness at hearing of his sad fate on the local news. There were a few comments about his incredible talent and questions about when his funeral would be.

She thought for a moment and then posted a message along with a lovely photo she had taken of Jimmy and Powie standing in front of an old rose covered stone cottage down by the lake.

"The loss of our dear friend Jimmy is devastating, but I want his friends to know his beloved dog is safe with me and he is doing okay. I will post details of a funeral or memorial service when I know more. Rest well Jimmy. I will miss you terribly."

Diane didn't look forward to talking to the police again. Her previous experience with law enforcement when she was a young teen had been horrible and she had a weird feeling that the officer in charge of Jimmy's investigation didn't like her. She reached for her phone and called the one foster parent who had changed her life.

"Hi Liz. It's Diane."

"Hello! I was thinking of you. Didn't you know that old guy who was found dead in his house over on King?"

"I was on my way to work and I got off the streetcar when I saw the emergency vehicles. I saw him on the stretcher covered with a blanket. I have his dog." She said in a shaking voice.

"I'm sorry. That's just awful. The news said they suspected foul play, whatever that means. You okay?"

"The police want to see me tomorrow. I already saw them this afternoon. Jimmy left me his estate and I'm scared Liz. I think they might suspect me."

"Just tell the truth honey. If you think you need a lawyer, I can get money from my credit line. Don't worry. I know you wouldn't hurt a fly."

"If they know I have a record for stealing, who knows what conclusions they'll jump to."

"Diane. Stop. You were a kid and you had no choice. Look what you did with your life! You went from being two years behind at school to graduating high school early with a full academic scholarship to a good university! I am more proud of you than I am of any other child I ever took in. You know that don't you?"

"It was all because of you Liz. You were my angel."

"Stay strong and stay calm. I will help you in any way I can. But now I have to go pick up the boys from soccer. I must be nuts. I took in ten year old twins! Come for dinner Sunday night okay?"

"I will. Love you."

Diane would never forget her fourteenth year. She was on family number six when she woke up to hear the sounds of a violent argument between her foster parents. She picked up her old teddy bear for comfort and when she poked her head out of her bedroom door to see what was happening, the heavyset man who reminded her daily that she was a "charity case", grabbed her and slammed her hard against the wall. She instinctively knew she had to get out and had run out onto the street wearing only a T-shirt and jeans. She had nothing but the clothes on her back but she knew she couldn't stay a minute longer. Surviving for days on food she saw being thrown out behind restaurants, she was determined not to go back to foster care despite the painful cuts on her bare feet. When she grabbed a pair of $2 flip flops from a display in front of a variety store and dashed away, the owner called the cops. She was apprehended and taken to the police station where she tried to tell the officers that her foster parents were abusive. After several hours, she was put in a van and transported to a center for delinquent teens. The only saving grace was that she was safe there and had access to the psychotherapy she was in desperate need of. Ten months later she was placed in foster care with Liz Collins who lived in a big old house close to the lake. There she had found the loving steady influence she had craved all of her life, and she flourished.

She had to stay calm like Liz said. She was innocent. Wasn't that all that mattered?

CHAPTER FOUR

Diane took a seat across from Scott Harris and a woman he had introduced as Officer Mills. There was a recorder on the table and a box of tissues.

"Well, Diane, here we are again." Scott said in what could only be described as a condescending tone.

"I'm not sure why you need to see me today. Have there been developments in Jimmy's case so soon?"

Officer Mills leaned forward, "Diane, where were you the morning of Mr. Freeman's death, between 7:00 and 9:00 a.m.?"

"I was at home. I left to go to work at the shelter at 10:10 to catch the 10:15 streetcar."

"Was anyone with you?"

"Just my three dogs and my cat."

"Can anyone verify that you were at home during that time period?"

Diane felt sweat starting to bead on her forehead. "Why are you asking me this? I found out about Jimmy's death when the streetcar stopped in front of his house. I saw you then." She answered looking straight at Scott.

"Yes. You were at the right place at the right time."

As she told herself to be calm, Diane felt her blood boiling.

"I told you, I was on my way to work."

"Weren't you worried about being late? There was a shuttle bus coming along to pick up people from the streetcar. You could've just gone on your way."

"I am an Animal Services employee and I heard a dog in distress. I knew that dog and it would have been unconscionable of me to leave him alone in a bad situation."

"So you knew it was a 'bad situation'?"

"No! I mean, I saw the emergency vehicles there so it was obvious something had happened and then when I got off the streetcar I saw Jimmy's body on the stretcher."

"How did you know it was him? The body was covered with a blanket."

"His dog was being held by one of your officers. He told me that the dog's owner was deceased."

Officer Mills stared at Diane for a moment and then asked;

"What exactly was the nature of your relationship with Mr. Freeman? How long had you known him and in what capacity?"

"I met Jimmy two years ago when he came to the shelter looking for a dog to adopt."

"How old would he have been at that time?"

"Seventy-three."

"Can you tell us what happened that day?"

"Well, Jimmy arrived at the same time as a nine year old dog was being brought in. His owner had died. They liked each other and so I allowed the adoption."

"Right then and there with no further investigation?"

"You have to understand, the shelter was at capacity. There was no room for the dog and he faced transfer to a place that most likely would have euthanized him due to his age. I had a sense about Jimmy and I just knew it would be okay."

"So you broke the rules."

"I arranged to follow up with a home visit the next day."

"Is that normal protocol?"

"No, but I wanted to make sure..."

"Basically, you sized up the situation. Old guy, all alone, owned a house..."

Diane read the contempt on the faces of the officers and felt a chill run down her spine.

"I just needed to make sure the dog would be okay. They were both really happy. Jimmy had given the dog a bath, bought him food, toys and a bed. I knew I had made the right decision."

"So why not leave it at that? Why start a relationship?"

"It was a friendship! Jimmy asked me to join them for walks in the park with my dogs and from there we became friends."

Scott smirked, "Two lonely souls..."

Diane crossed her arms in front of her and blinked back tears.

"I'm not playing this game. I had nothing to do with Jimmy's death. If I should hire a lawyer, I will do that, but I'm not talking to you anymore."

She was told she was free to leave but she felt like she was in a virtual jail cell as she ran out of the building. She stopped, breathing in the irony of the perfectly beautiful day as she frantically hailed a cab to take her home. The dogs met her at the door and she buried her face in their soft hair and sobbed, crying out;

"Jimmy what on earth happened?"

Hearing Jimmy's name, Powie ran over to Diane and licked her face. She gently pushed him down and kissed his head.

"I love you sweetie, but right now I just want you to speak to me in English and tell me who hurt your daddy."

When the dog responded by scratching at his neck, Diane checked his collar to see if it was too tight. She noticed that a square had been cut in the fabric and sewn up with mismatched thread.

"What happened to your beautiful collar? Jimmy loved this batik pattern." She remembered when they had bought the collar at an arts and crafts fair in the park by the beach. She had joked about how Powie now matched with his owner's Bohemian style.

She picked at the thread that was coming loose and realized that there was something behind the cloth. After a few tugs, the fabric lifted up to reveal a small piece of paper folded tightly. As she opened the note, a tiny silver key fell into her hand. The words on the note were printed precisely in blue pen,

"Key to the V".

What on earth? Diane put the note and the key into a jar in her kitchen cupboard and figured she would have an infinitesimal chance of ever finding out what it was for. She just wanted this day to be over, but at the same time, she feared what tomorrow would bring.

That afternoon, at the police station, Scott Harris handed his partner a cup of coffee and wondered out loud if he should've found a way to detain Diane Daniels.

"Release the body, give her the keys to the house and watch her like a hawk. She's going to break. The prints that were lifted off the cup she handled here yesterday do not match the ones on the beer bottle that was used to kill Freeman, but there were also smudges on the bottle consistent with someone handling it while wearing gloves. We can't hold her until we have something. You know that. But she's got opportunist written all over her. Beautiful young woman, lonely old man…"

"I guess we have limited options right now. I agree with you though. She will crack." Officer Mills picked up the file folder and sighed. "Poor old fellow didn't deserve this."

The next few weeks rushed by and as the flowers started blooming in the gardens, Diane took possession of Jimmy's house. She held a gathering of remembrance in his favorite park with a group of the musician's friends and neighbors who fed the squirrels and the birds while his nearest and dearest played guitar and sang "Wonderful World". It was touching and heartfelt and Diane knew Jimmy would have been happy to be remembered outside, with the sun shining and the birds singing.

Now she was feeling almost overwhelmed by the tasks at hand. The house was full of boxes, trunks and suitcases that contained the items Jimmy had collected through the years. Every room revealed a different era of his life. The bedroom was overflowing with clothes. Diane sorted things and dropped most of them off at a local charity. In a bottom drawer she found an envelope of photos of Jimmy that were taken by a photographer in Nashville. She remembered him telling her about the photo he had given to his friend Janet. He looked so different, but his twinkly bright blue eyes were the same. She packed up the kitchen and donated the useable things to a second hand store. The musical items were plentiful and she was confused as to how to deal with the boxes of old tapes, binders full of lyric sheets, recording equipment and a couple of keyboards that looked like they might be worth something. She decided to call Lucas for advice as he was in the music business and had offered to help when she had seen him at the memorial. They agreed to meet at the house on the weekend to sort through the music room.

Diane had been going to the house on the way home from work every night and it was usually after dark when she locked up and crossed the road to wait for the streetcar. As she stood at the dimly lit stop just after dusk, she noticed a beat up old car pull up in front of Jimmy's house. A man got out of the vehicle, glanced around quickly and then stealthily made his way up to the front door. He didn't knock, but Diane could see he tried to turn the doorknob. Seeing it was locked, he shone the light from his phone at the window that still displayed Jimmy's photo collection. It appeared that he took a photo, but Diane couldn't be sure. She wondered if she should call out to the visitor and see why he was there but something held her back. The man next walked to the side of the house. Diane quietly moved forward so that she could have a better view of the property. The stranger went to the window that would lead into the bedroom and pushed on it just as the next-door neighbor came out onto his porch and looked around. The unknown man stayed in the shadows until all was clear and then went back to his car and drove away. Diane was unnerved. This was the type of thing you called and reported to the police, but she couldn't do that after the way they had treated her like a suspect in Jimmy's murder. She was relieved when the streetcar arrived and she was finally on her way home.

CHAPTER FIVE

Lucas arrived at the house just after 6:00 p.m. on a warm Sunday night as they had planned earlier in the week. He was a keyboard player who had been Jimmy's closest friend for the past ten years. At sixty-five he liked to joke that he could pass for forty if it was dark enough. He'd been married to the same woman for thirty years, which was a record in his circle, and he had told Diane he felt very lost without his best pal. It turned out that the keyboards were hand-me-downs he had given Jimmy but he was happy to take them back for his grandson. The tapes were going to take time to sort through so he carefully packed them in a plastic crate along with the binders full of sheet music and lyrics. There was still a lot to do but Lucas told Diane he had to have dinner on schedule due to his Type 2 diabetes and the pair decided to go to a local café for a sandwich and coffee. After they had settled in at a table by the window, Lucas told Diane he was completely perplexed about the killing of his friend.

"Do you think it could've been one of the bad characters from the neighborhood asking him for money and it just went wrong?" Diane asked.

"He would've given them something they could sell if he didn't have cash. He was so easy with people. I think it had to be a lot more serious."

"Do you think he had a secret we weren't aware of like gambling debts or something?"

"I really don't think so. But there are crazy people out there. He didn't have much of value except the house. That guitar he left me is worth about $500. You never know though. There were rumors that Jimmy had a rare old guitar, but I never saw it and I'm sure it was long gone. It might've been what he used to come up with a down payment for his house. He was thrifty but he did pretty well for someone living on pensions."

Lucas ordered more coffee and smiled at his young companion.

"The most important thing to Jimmy was that dog. He brought him back to life. If someone had threatened Powie, he would've fought back."

"Are you game for another hour or so of packing? I want to get as much out of there as possible. After I left the last time, a man pulled up in an old car and it looked like he was trying to open the door. People know the house is empty and they could come looking for an opportunity…"

"The manager from the music store on Grey Ave. drives an old car and I wouldn't put it past him to come skulking around. If there is anything to be sold, he's going to want to help you out, if you know what I mean? Let's pay this bill and get back at it. Once the stuff is cleared out, I can help you with the cleaning that hasn't been done in twenty years! Then if anybody breaks in they won't be quite as horrified!"

Diane and Lucas worked in the house until just after 10:00 p.m. and then he dropped her off at home. She had saved some of Jimmy's brightly patterned scarves for him and he had one wrapped around his head Keith Richard's style for the drive home.

"I think I should take the tapes over to Marty Cohen, he's a recording engineer and see if there is anything we can work with. I'm really excited about this! Makes me feel like a young rock star again!"

"Your wife is going to hate me!" Diane called out as she waved good-bye. She was grateful for not only the help but also the company. Lucas had made her laugh and it was a good feeling.

Scott Harris was working the night shift and decided to catch up on any developments in the unsolved case dossier that sat prominently on his desk. He pulled out the Jimmy Freeman file and realized it had been almost five months since the man had been killed and there was still no progress in the investigation. Diane Daniels had submitted all of the paperwork necessary to have the will probated and she was cleaning out the house, preparing it for sale on the fall market. He had not talked to her since the day when she had abruptly ended their interview, but she remained his primary suspect.

The local paper had run a story about the memorial held in the park for the victim. It was a sunshine and rainbows kind of spectacle with a couple of old geezers playing off key tunes on their beat up guitars. He knew, because he had observed the whole thing from the street. Diane had held court in a flowered dress with a daisy chain in her hair. Could it get more cliché? Throw in half a dozen hipster musicians with tattoos and man-buns who showed up to pay their "respect" and it was enough to make him sick. He just wanted to put this one to rest. The area was going through a gentrification and it was important to make the residents feel safe. An unsolved murder in their midst was concerning and the pressure was on him to wrap it up. He put a reminder in his calendar to stop by the house in the next week. Diane must be getting comfortable by now and that was when most slip-ups occurred.

CHAPTER SIX

A week after their packing frenzy, Lucas called Diane and asked her to come to the recording studio run by his friend Marty Cohen. He told her there was something she needed to hear and he was leaving it at that. After the dogs were walked and she had spent time playing with her cat, she hopped on the subway and made the trip out to the west end. It was a warm late summer evening and many couples were out walking hand in hand or enjoying coffee and conversation at the numerous outdoor cafes. She felt a pang of loneliness. She had dated off and on throughout her adult years but had never felt strongly enough about anyone to enter into a long-term relationship. She wondered if she would ever have a life that revolved around humans as much as it did around animals. Just as she was turning up the street where the studio was located, she heard her name being called out.

"Diane! Over here!"

Lucas sat at an outside table at a small Mexican restaurant with a man who was closer to her age than his and a very large, very shaggy sheepdog.

"Glad I spotted you! You know me and the meal plan! This is Marty, and his dog, Hendrix."

Marty stood up and extended his hand. He was about six foot two with long braided hair tied back with what looked to be one of Jimmy's scarves. He stared at Lucas with a quizzical expression and said;

"Sorry, I'm kind of blindsided here. Lucas had me thinking Jimmy's friend was going to be a grey-haired lady in her seventies. Please join us, it's such a nice night we felt we had to take advantage of it."

They decided unanimously to enjoy some nachos, quesadillas and Sangria before heading into the studio. Hendrix, who was tied to the wrought iron fence beside their table, stayed fast asleep until the food came and then sat up and stared longingly at the platters on the table.

"So, how familiar are you with Jimmy's music? Ever see him play?" Marty asked Diane.

"He'd play his guitar for me sometimes and he had such a great voice, but whenever I asked him to play me the music he had recorded years ago, he dodged the subject."

"There was still a lot of pain there, even though he looked like he had it all resolved. He told me once that he just had to accept that he would never get the recognition he deserved. But he didn't have to like it."

They left soon after and Diane was surprised at how opulent the furnishings of the studio were considering how unassuming it looked from the street. She was directed to a teal leather sofa that was beautifully accented by a vibrant Persian rug and polished rosewood bookshelves. Marty went into the studio and came out with a remote control.

"Ready?"

"I guess." She smiled.

The room then filled with the sound of an acoustic guitar and Jimmy's voice singing a song about the destruction of his neighborhood.

"They're tearing down God's house on the corner
Making way for glass and chrome
I'm kneeling in the shadows praying
No one hears me
No one's home
Going to take that stained-glass window
Hang it like some art so fine
I'll have a church right in my kitchen
And call the angel's party line
There's a choir in my attic
Incense in the air
I've got some wine and a candle
And my faith is what I wear..."

The engineer, Lucas and several other studio musicians had taken Jimmy's latest tape and produced a stunning version of something the elderly bluesman had casually written on his front porch while he watched unique old buildings razed to be replaced by modern structures with no imagination. Diane brushed her tears away.

"He would be so proud! It's wonderful."

Marty breathed a sigh of relief and clapped his hands in triumph.

"When Lucas told me about your friendship with Jimmy and how you brought that sweet old dog into his life, I wanted you to approve. We're going to release a CD with ten songs as a tribute. They'll all have to be reworked, but I can isolate his vocals and clean them up. There are some really great tunes there. I just love one called "After the Dance…" and of course we have to use "Powder, baby!"

"I know that one!" Diane laughed. "It was about his 'bromance' with Powie. He couldn't get through it without the dog howling like a back-up singer and he'd crack up laughing."

"That's what that is on the freakin' tape! I kept listening to it thinking it was his fridge humming or something. That's one weird sounding dog!"

Lucas sat back quietly watching the start of a new friendship. He really liked both of these people and he was happy that they were getting along so well. Diane was a good soul and he loved Marty like a son. This would make his old pal smile.

Marty said he wanted Diane to hear "After the dance…" even though it was pretty rough, he thought she'd like it. When the song ended he punched Lucas lightly on the arm.

"Man that 'V' sure had a sweet sound didn't she?"

"Rumor has it, he still had her but I never saw it in all the years I knew him and you never found it did you Diane?"

Diane shook her head in confusion. "What was I supposed to find?"

"The Flying V!" Marty and Lucas said in unison.

"A very rare, extremely valuable, 1959 electric guitar." Lucas finished.

"Key to the V". Diane whispered.

"What?" Lucas leaned forward.

"Maybe you two can make sense of this. I found a key sewn into Powie's collar, with a note that said "Key to the V".

"Oh crap! He's hidden it somewhere!" Lucas shouted as the two men howled with laughter at the absurdity of such an important instrument going missing.

"Is it really valuable?"

Marty sighed. "Only worth over a quarter of a million."

Lucas offered to drive Diane home and on the way they tossed around ideas as to where the guitar might be.

"The old kook may have it stashed in a locker at the bus terminal for all we know!"

"The attic is full of insulation. I already looked up there to ensure it was clear."

"This may remain a mystery. Damn!"

Diane gave Lucas a hug and promised to call him to make arrangements to get the heavy items out of the house. Marty had offered the use of his truck which would be helpful in getting an old bench and trunk that she wanted to keep, over to her house. She waved goodbye and smiled as she noticed that he didn't drive away until she was safely inside. She changed her clothes and then went to her cupboard and took out the little key and the note that had been wrapped around it.

'Key to the V'. Where on earth could he have hidden it?

She had cleaned right through the kitchen and the living room and bedroom were totally emptied out except for the couple of large items she had decided to keep. There seemed like nowhere to hide something as big as a guitar. She and Lucas had agreed to scour the place once again, but she couldn't imagine where it could be in that little house. The backyard was tiny and there were no outer buildings so she was at a loss as to where Jimmy would've hidden it. She called to the dogs to come to bed and fell asleep with all four and the cat snuggled together.

CHAPTER SEVEN

The decision to take Powie to the house for one final visit was a last minute one. He had looked at her strangely when she had said out loud that she was going to his daddy's house to get the remaining things out before it was to be put on the market. Something in his eyes made her think it would be good for him to see that the place he most likely remembered as home, no longer had Jimmy there. When they arrived, the dog quivered with excitement but after sniffing his way through the rooms, he seemed to accept that his old friend was gone. His moment of sadness passed quickly though and he almost knocked Marty flat on his back when he came through the door. The recording engineer had pulled his truck into the laneway behind the house, oblivious to the watchful eyes of a man sitting a half a block away in a rusted-out sedan.

"Jimmy never taught him not to jump on people and I'm afraid I'm failing miserably too!" Diane apologized.

"He's fine. He just needs a ball to chase or something."

The dog raised one ear, looked at Marty as if he had spoken in code and dashed into the back bedroom. Diane was about to offer Marty a cold drink when the sound of Powie madly scratching at something, prompted her to investigate.

"Pow! What are you doing? There's nothing there." She said as she tried to pull the dog out of the small closet. He whined and broke away from her to return to the exact spot he had been ripping at a moment before.

"What is it Buddy? " Marty shone the flashlight from his cell phone into the corner. "Looks like something metal there. Do you see what I mean?"

Diane bent down and pulled on the little metal ring that was illuminated by the light. A trap door opened and she jumped back. Marty moved in and lifted out a dusty guitar case locked with a tiny padlock.

"The Flying V!" They said laughing together. Powie dove into the space where the guitar had been and emerged with a worn tennis ball.

"That's what he was looking for! He must've remembered that his ball dropped in with the guitar the last time Jimmy took it out. Take it to the kitchen. There are some dust cloths there. I'm going to close this up."

Diane pushed the trap door closed and called Powie to come with her. Steps from the kitchen, the dog began to bark and Diane could see Marty standing against the counter with his hands raised in front of him. The man she had seen casing the house a few weeks before, was holding a gun and demanding that he open the case.

"I don't have the key." Marty stated in a trembling voice.

Diane tried to make a run for it so she could get help but the man grabbed her by the arm and jabbed his gun into her ribs.

"I knew that guitar was here all along. Jimmy almost sold it to me once. Too bad the old fool didn't take my last offer. He'd still be alive."

Diane squirmed as she tried to free herself.

"You killed him! Why did you have to kill him?!"

The man hissed at her, "I hate waste. He wasn't going to make use of the value in that guitar so I told him I'd make use of it myself. I could live down in South America for the rest of my life off of that Flying V. He told me to get out, as if I wasn't good enough to be in his crappy little house. He always thought he was better than the rest of us! Told me the guitar wasn't here! Going senile if you ask me. I just took a step to go take a look for myself and he tried to block me. That made me angry, so I hit him with the bottle I was carrying. Is that enough for you pretty lady?"

Marty had stayed put but had managed to get his hand into his pocket where he had put his cell phone while Diane distracted the intruder. He didn't want to place her in more danger than she was already in by trying to escape. Recognizing the man as the manager of a local music store, who was also an ex-con, he knew not to mess with him. But, he also knew dogs, and how they protected those they loved. He looked at Powie and then looked frantically over at Diane. The dog stared at him for a long moment, head cocked to one side as if reading his mind and then launched himself full force at the chest of the murderer while letting out a shriek loud enough to break glass. The gun flew out of the killer's hand as he fell back letting go of Diane. Marty grabbed the firearm and pointed it at the man who was now lying helpless on the floor.

"C'mon friend. You don't want to shoot me. You're in the business too. You understand…" the criminal pleaded in a pathetic tone, as he looked nervously at the dog who stood over him growling.

"Stop talking and don't try my patience." Marty stated with a no nonsense air.

It was only minutes before the police arrived in response to Diane's frantic call to 911. They were surprised to find that their work had been done for them in the form of the taped "confession" Marty had captured on his cell phone while the killer described the events that had resulted in Jimmy Freeman's death.

Later that day, Diane and Marty met with Scott Harris at the police Station to give their formal statements shortly after the arrest was made and Powie had been returned home to sleep off the excitement.

The police official stared at the paperwork in front of him and appeared almost sheepish.

Diane leaned forward forcing Scott to look at her.

"You really thought I was guilty didn't you? The man who killed Jimmy Freeman had a criminal record. He'd been to the house before. Didn't his prints put off some kind of alarm or were you just too busy looking at me?"

"It looked that way Miss Daniels. I was wrong."

He would never admit that the murderer's fingerprints did come up, but after a brief interview with the music shop manager he had dropped him a as suspect. The ex-con had told him that he had been in and out of the house on a weekly basis for years "helping" Jimmy and that there were always beer bottles on the counter. He had laughed when asked about Jimmy's sobriety.

"Sober? Seriously? He had a beer for breakfast, tequila for lunch and rye for supper."

That was enough to convince the officer who had already mentally convicted the young woman who had appeared at just the right time.

It was about as close to an apology as she was going to get. Marty sensed her frustration and put his arm around her as they left the station.

"Well honey, that was a pretty wild first date! Could we just go out and have dinner now?"

Diane laughed and leaned in against her new friend. She suggested they get Chinese food at a family run restaurant over by her place. As she opened her fortune cookie after their meal, Marty took the message out of her hand;

"Fortune says; you will sell a rare guitar and use the money to start a rescue organization for older dogs. A ridiculously handsome recording engineer will assist you. You will be very happy."

"I was thinking, 'Freeman's Best Friend Dog Rescue'. No pun intended, but it works."

"That's the best thing I've heard in a long time. When do we start?"

FREEMAN'S BEST FRIEND
DOG RESCUE

A Rescue Dog Mystery
By: Michele Anne O'Neail

CHAPTER ONE

Diane Daniels reached over two dogs to answer her phone which was ringing off the hook at 5:30 a.m.

"Hello?"

"Diane. It's Marty. Sorry to call you so early but I wanted to let you know before I got on the plane. I'm bringing that little dog I told you about last week. I managed to get her shots done and clearance to fly. She really needs us."

"What time do you get in? I can pick you up."

"It's Air Canada from Kingston due in at 10:30. That would be great if you could come. I missed you."

"Missed you too. I'll come in to arrivals. Have a safe flight."

Diane yawned and made a futile attempt to stretch out her legs. Her Maltese was asleep on the pillow beside her, her German Shepard was sprawled close to the edge of the bed and her Labradoodle and Bearded Collie were flopped across her legs. Marty's Old English Sheepdog lay on the floor beside the door. She loved them all dearly, but sleeping with them was difficult to say the least. Katie, the littlest one rolled over and snuggled against her neck.

"Let's sleep for a little while longer guys. Mommy's tired."

The alarm went off to a chorus of barking two hours later and the group made their way to the kitchen and then out the back door. Diane prepared meals for the pack and quietly fed her little blind tabby cat under the table. It was chaos at times, but she loved it. Abbie, the German Shepard, was born with only three legs and although she didn't know she was different from the others, she had some difficulties resulting from extra strain on her existing back limb and needed anti-inflammatory medicine. The Maltese, Katie, was almost totally deaf and would linger in the yard unless she saw the others going in and would follow them. Albert, a Bearded Collie was diabetic and needed insulin shots twice a day and strictly monitored food intake. The least of her problems was Powie, an almost twelve-year-old Labradoodle who had come to live with her when his owner was sadly murdered a year ago. He had no discernible health problems and his sweet nature made up for his lack of formal training. He loved playing with Hendrix when he stayed over and the pair, were never seen without a ball or a rope toy. She wondered what the story was with the little dog Marty was brining back from his trip to Jamaica. He had gone there for his annual visit with his mother who had been in and out of his life while he was growing up and had finally gone back to the Island as she was happier there. Both Marty and Diane were kids who had gone through "the system" and their shared knowledge of life as displaced children had created a serious bond between them.

When Diane had found herself to be the unexpected heir of blues musician Jimmy Freeman's surprisingly ample estate, she had been able to buy a small house down by the lake that had originally been a summer cottage. The home was rustic and cozy and although the kitchen and bathroom had been renovated, the place still had the ambiance of a country retreat, and a leaky roof to confirm its authenticity. The fenced backyard was perfect for the dogs and she loved the wild garden that was the front lawn. She had also purchased a van for the dog rescue she and Marty Cohen had started with the proceeds of the auction of an extremely rare guitar they had discovered under the floorboards in Jimmy›s house. A discovery that had almost gotten them both killed. But that was another story.

She secured the first aid kit in the backseat along with a tiny seatbelt for the new arrival and drove through horrendous traffic from the east end of the city to the airport which was in the far west. Throngs of passengers crowded the terminal as she made her way to arrivals. There was the usual assortment of travellers returning home from sun drenched beach vacations and honeymoons. Marty, at six foot two, long braided hair swinging as he strode quickly through the last Customs checkpoint stuck out not as much for his rock star looks this day as he did for the ear piercing shrieking coming from the small dog kennel he carried and the look of outright exasperation on his handsome face.

"She's been screaming since we left the plane. I don't dare open the carrier until we get her in the car. I have no idea what's wrong!"

He gave Diane a kiss on the cheek and said with a smile "Look how you've complicated my life."

As soon as they got to the van, Diane pulled the kennel into the back seat with her and opened the door. The tiniest little face peered out at her.

"Come here sweetie." Diane whispered as she reached in to pull the dog out.

"Look at you. You have such pretty eyes."

The dog weighed about five pounds if that and looked very neglected. She smelled terrible and was shaking.

"You drive. Take us straight to the Animal Hospital. I think she's in pretty bad shape. What do you know about her?"

"I saw her begging for food around the resort. One of the maids told me she first showed up about a year ago and was surviving on scraps from the restaurant. When I saw one of the maintenance guys kicking her I grabbed her and took her to my room. She escaped the first time I opened the door so I couldn't really assess her condition, then the day before yesterday I heard that they were trying to catch her so she could be put down. There are a few dogs that hang around because they know the tourists give them treats and the people that run the place don't like it. I lured her with some chicken and she seemed to like me after that. I took her to a vet who charged an arm and a leg for a basic rabies shot and here we are."

"She looks like a Yorkie. I wonder how she ever ended up there."

"There are a lot of stray dogs in the streets in Jamaica. It's not like here. They can survive due to the climate and they just aren't thought of as pets. It's really sad. How's my boy?"

"He's fine. Powie loves having him around. Me too."

When they arrived at the Animal Hospital, the veterinary assistant took the kennel from Diane and asked for information about the dog.

"Name?"

Marty shrugged his shoulders. I've been calling her "Sweetie" for lack of a real name.

"Country of origin?"

"Jamaica. She's had her rabies shot. Here's the paperwork."

"Okay, let's take a look."

The dog looked even more pathetic now that she was under the bright lights of the clinic and her infected eyes and ears were exposed. She had severely dirty, matted hair and nails that looked like they hadn't been cut in ages. The Veterinarian joined them and gently examined her while she shook her head.

"I don't have to do an X-Ray to tell you she has broken ribs. I just have to do one to see how bad it is. You said you picked her up in Jamaica?"

"Yes. She was hanging around a resort there and she was going to be trapped and put down." Marty advised.

"It will take me a couple of hours to check her out and clean her up. Why don't you guys come back at 3:00 ?"

"We'll go get lunch and come back. Thanks for seeing her so quickly."

At the coffee shop just down the road, over crepes with Brie and pear, Marty filled Diane in about his trip.

"It was good to see my mother finally healthy and in a good, solid relationship. Wish she could've managed that when I was a kid."

Diane smiled at the man who had slowly over the past year become very important to her.

"Just be happy you have her. And it sounds like you ate well while you were there. Every time you called me you were on your way out to lunch or dinner!"

"I must have gained twenty pounds! The aunties get insulted if you don't eat so it was 'curried this' and 'jerk that', not to mention the rum cake!"

Time passed quickly and they were soon back at the clinic to pick up "Sweetie". While they waited, one of the technicians came out to talk to them.

"We cleaned her up as best we could. Two ribs are broken and she had an abscess, beneath one of her really bad mats. She's going to need medication for the pain and for her eyes and ears. And, she's micro-chipped. Twice actually. We could see the chips on the x-ray and when we scanned her, one of them gave us the registration identification number and the chip company to call in Seattle. The other chip seems to be sending out information that can't be read."

Diane looked puzzled. "Does this mean she's from Washington State?"

"Probably that part of the world. The company is a smaller one so she was most likely on the U.S West Coast when she was chipped. Kind of weird about the second chip though, I've never encountered that before."

"Can we take her home?" Marty asked.

"Give us a day. We want to manage her pain well and get her on the road to recovery. You did a good thing. She probably wouldn't have survived for much longer. She's really undernourished and dehydrated."

CHAPTER TWO

Hendrix was overjoyed to see his dad and managed to position his ninety-pound self on Marty's lap with his big paws around his neck. The sheep dog had been for sale online when his photo had inadvertently popped up while Marty was searching for a brand of old English lemon oil he used to polish the furniture and cabinets in his studio. He had a strange feeling that the dog needed him and he had driven out to a farm north of the city and taken the large, shaggy guy home that night. They bonded almost immediately and he couldn't imagine life without his best friend.

"I'll call that microchip company tomorrow morning. I doubt we'll find out anything but it's worth a shot." Diane called out from the kitchen where she was dividing kibble between five bowls and refilling the water dishes.

"I'm trying to figure out how a dog from the west coast of the states could end up in Jamaica. But I guess it could happen. Maybe someone brought her there and she took off and they couldn't find her. The maid I talked to said that she just appeared on the beach one day and started hanging around. She was really scared and wouldn't go to anyone. She must've had a place she hid and just came out to find food because she was around for quite a while."

"She's going to have to be fostered in a calm home. Maybe Liz will take her. She has no other pets there right now and the boys are really good with animals, so I wouldn't be worried."

Marty frowned in concern. "Does Liz really like me?" He asked about the woman who had been Diane's foster mother and the person who was instrumental in making the young woman the grounded, loving person she was today.

"Yeah. She does. She said once she got past the dreadlocks..."

"You mean my braids? That's hilarious!"

"She really does like you. If she didn't, she would never ask you to dinner." Diane smiled. "Liz is very definite in her opinions. I'll call her later and see if she can take Sweetie."

Later that evening, Diane made arrangements with her former foster mom, Liz, to take Sweetie when she was discharged from the veterinary clinic on Monday morning. It was the best situation for the sick little dog. Liz was a very kind person and she was home all day which meant that the tiny Yorkie would get the attention she needed to regain her health and learn to trust humans again. The eleven-year-old twin boys who were currently being fostered by Liz were more than happy to help with the care and training that was going to be needed. Knowing that her latest "rescue" was going to be okay, Diane drove to the building she had bought and renovated along with Marty. They had needed a space that would be able to accommodate numerous dogs who were waiting for appropriate foster homes or adoptive parents. With a lot of hard work, they had managed to create a place that was functional but was also a warm, safe and happy environment for the mostly senior dogs they took on freedom rides from over filled shelters. They currently were housing twelve dogs between the ages of eight and thirteen. All were cared for by volunteers who only wanted the best for them.

The one who pulled on her heartstrings the most was Macy, a nine-year-old Bouvier des Flandres who had been surrendered when her family decided to move to Europe. She seemed completely lost and confused at first and Diane was spending as much time with her as was possible in the hope that she could possibly be integrated into her own pack of dogs. Before going to see her though, she went into her office and retrieved Sweetie's microchip information from the slip of paper she had stashed in her purse. She dialed the long distance number and was quickly connected to an operator who asked for the unique identification number that was attached to the microchip.

"You are a rescue organization, right?"

"Yes. We're called Freeman's Best Friend Dog Rescue and we are located in Toronto, Canada. My name is Diane Daniels and I am trying to establish the identity of a little Yorkie who was found in Jamaica. She was in danger and my colleague brought her here to Canada to save her life. Our veterinary clinic scanned for a chip and there are actually two implanted in her. One was readable and connected us to you."

Once the number was provided, the operator put Diane on hold and was gone for a few minutes. When she returned she spoke in a conspiratorial tone.

"There has been no payment to our company for the last two years. The dog was chipped in Seattle. The information we have is sketchy. She is listed as a Yorkie-Poo and her name is Maggie. There is just a phone number. No name and address, which is really strange. I guess you could call. We don't follow up when the account has lapsed for more than two years and we are at the twenty-eight month point with no contact and no payment on this registration. This normally happens when a dog has died. If a dog goes missing, the owners usually ensure that they keep the chip active in case someone finds the pet. I'm sorry I can't be more helpful."

Diane took down the phone number attached to Maggie and thanked the operator for at least giving the little dog back her name. She made a pot of coffee and called Liz.

"Hi! Say hello to Maggie for me."

"Oh! That's wonderful! You've found her family then?" Liz asked.

"Not exactly. The chip has kind of lapsed as far as payment goes, but I did get the last phone number associated with her. It's for Seattle Washington though, so I have to wait to call as it is too early right now."

"How on earth did she end up in Jamaica? Well call me when you know more. She's doing great and is the gentlest little thing. I guess the fact she is a Yorkie-Poo explains her curly hair! I wouldn't mind keeping her if you can't find her family."

"Thanks Liz. You truly are the best. I will call you as soon as I know anything."

Diane waited a couple of hours and then dialed the phone number in Seattle. It was out of service. She then called the phone company and was told, as she had expected, that no information about the number could be released due to confidentiality issues. She called Liz and told her she Was getting nowhere fast. She went to Macy's kennel and let the big old dog out. Macy rubbed her head on Diane's leg and stayed as close as she possibly could to the woman who had driven her through pouring rain to the place where she had had to adjust to a new reality without the family she had known all of her life. If she could've talked she would have let Diane know that she had been comfortable before, but had never had someone pay the kind of attention to her that she was now getting, and she loved it.

Diane put a leash on Macy and walked her over to Marty's studio, which was just down the block. Hendrix was playing with a ball in the fenced in front yard of the converted house and ran over to meet them, tail wagging and tongue hanging out.

"Hi big fellow! Meet Macy. Finally someone your size!"

The two dogs sniffed each other and then lay down side by side. Instant friends. Dogs were funny that way. If they sensed a kinship, they would bond immediately. Diane let herself into the studio and made her way down the hall to the kitchen area as she could hear voices coming from there.

"I left Macy outside with Hendrix. That's okay?"

"He'll love the company. Meet Jesse, my latest discovery!" Marty smiled gesturing to a young man who didn't look more than sixteen. "This guy has a voice you just have to hear!"

"Hi. Nice to meet you. Do you have a dog too?" The shy boy asked.

"Dogs plural. The one I left out front is a rescue. She's needing some TLC so I take her out for walks when I can."

"Mark my words, that big old girl is going to be a foster fail. You are going to keep her." Marty laughed.

"That would be dog number five. I think there is a city bylaw against that!"

Diane updated Marty on the information she had found on little "Maggie" and made a date for dinner later. She felt they both needed some time away from all of their pets so they could talk without interruption. She had really missed him when he was away and it kind of unnerved her as she prided herself on her independence and her ability to take care of herself. She went back outside to find Macy, looking happy and relaxed, sitting on the steps beside her new friend.

When Diane and Marty had opened Freeman's Best Friend Dog Rescue they knew there would be some heartbreaking moments, but they had forged ahead with the plan they had formulated in a relatively short period of time. They purchased a building close to Marty's studio as the neighbourhood was still offering real estate for a fair price and it was an area that was being gentrified, which meant it was quickly becoming dog-centric. The amount of time they spent arranging for freedom-rides for the "un-adoptable", veterinary care, foster homes, not to mention purchasing supplies and fundraising was at times daunting, but they carried on for Jimmy Freeman, the man who had inspired it all.

Diane took Macy back to the rescue headquarters and phoned Liz. She explained that she had hit a dead end with the phone number attached to Maggie's microchip. She felt a bit discouraged but the fact that the tiny dog was doing well and would now have a chance for a good life made up for any frustration she was experiencing.

Liz administered Maggie's medications and gave the little dog a liver treat which she gobbled up like she would never get another one.

"Maggie, you didn't get to Jamaica all by yourself. There has to be a way to find out what happened and how."

Taking her tablet out on to her back porch, she started entering information into Google.

Lost Yorkie/Poo Seattle.

Nothing.

Lost Yorkie dog Ocho Rios Jamaica.

The name "Cassidy Stuart" came up. Google was weird, she thought.

Seattle area dog lost in Jamaica.

"Cassidy Stuart" came up again, this time with the qualifying term, "death notice".

It was too much of a coincidence so she clicked on it and a photo of a lovely young woman in a wedding dress, holding a dog looking very much like little Maggie, appeared.

"Cassidy Stuart, twenty-five, pictured above with her beloved Yorkie dog, Maggie, died tragically in Ocho Rios Jamaica. Recently married to John Porter, Cassidy Stuart also leaves behind her sister, Chelsea Stuart of Oak Hills, nieces Avalon and Annie and many friends and relatives. Service details follow..."

Liz felt a chill as she read the obituary. The dog in the photo could very well be the pup asleep beside her. If her owner had died while on vacation, she might've become confused and run off. She decided to send the link to Diane and let her figure out if an attempt at contact with the husband or sister should take place.

Diane phoned Liz immediately upon receiving the email with the link to Cassidy Stuart's obituary.

"It really looks like her. Did you by any chance find a number for the husband or the sister?"

"Yes I actually did. I have Chelsea Stuart's number. I think you should phone her. I wouldn't want to call the husband, it could be too upsetting."

"Agreed. I will call her. Text me the number."

The phone in the house in Oak Hills Washington owned by Chelsea Stuart, an interior designer, rang six times before it was answered.

"Hello. Chelsea Stuart."

"Hi, Miss Stuart. My name is Diane Daniels and I run a dog rescue in Toronto, Canada. I have reason to believe we may have found your sister's dog, Maggie."

"Is this some kind of sick joke? My sister died trying to save Maggie and they both drowned."

There was anger in the woman's voice and Diane felt like she had just opened Pandora's Box.

"I am so sorry, but my partner found a little dog in Ocho Rios last week and brought her home as she was in really bad shape. Her microchip was no longer active but was linked to a phone number in Seattle, and her name is Maggie."

There was a long silence.

"Cassidy drowned trying to save her dog. Her husband tried to save her but couldn't and he said he saw Maggie drown. He saw her drift off and he couldn't get her out of the water."

"I know this must sound crazy but the photo of your sister on her obituary...well the dog she's holding, it looks just like the dog we have here." Diane said quietly.

"You said there was a phone number attached to the chip. Do you have it?"

"It's 555-998-1334."

"Oh God! That's Cassidy and John's old number! She must've survived somehow. Can you email me a photo? I want to see her!"

"Of course! I'll send you something right away. She's going to be ok.

She must have just lived by her wits all this time and then started hanging around a beach resort where she could get food. She had some broken ribs so she's at a foster home getting really good care. Do you think your sister's husband will want her?"

"I'll let him know. He lives in Texas now. We really haven't been in touch lately."

"I'll send you a photo in the next few hours." Diane exchanged email addresses with Maggie's "aunt" and ended the call. She had not asked Chelsea if she would take Maggie if the widower didn't want her. It was all too soon and too raw. Liz was elated when she heard the news about locating Maggie's family.

"I just took a bunch of pictures of her. She is such a cutie! I'll send them to you now."

Diane laughed when no less than fifteen photos of the little dog popped up on her phone. Liz was a really good choice to foster Maggie. She had the ability to be fully engaged in the care and nurture of a child or pet, but could also manage to let them go if a positive permanent situation came along. Diane selected three of the best pictures and emailed them to Chelsea Stuart who immediately responded with a message;

"That's her! I know it's her! This is amazing!"

CHAPTER THREE

"John, it's Chelsea."

"Why are you calling me? It's been quite a while..."

"It's Maggie. She's been found!"

"Chelsea. Maggie drowned just like Cass. I couldn't save either one of them and you know that as well as I do."

"No! She didn't drown. It must've looked like that but she was found in pretty bad shape in Ocho Rios last week, and a man who runs a dog rescue shelter in Canada, made arrangements to take her there. Her microchip had your old phone number and her name. The people up there were determined to find her family, if there was one, and they connected her to Cassidy's online death notice and called me out of the blue."

The line was quiet for a moment and then John asked,

"This is unbelievable. What do we do?"

"Well, I'm thinking of taking her, unless you want to. I guess I should've thought of that option but she was Cassidy's before you met and I know you've moved on with your life."

Chelsea fought hard to keep the edge out of her voice. She knew John was now married and his new wife was expecting a baby. He had taken what seemed like seconds to move from utter devastation at the loss of his wife to a state of domestic bliss once again.

"Chelsea. I loved your sister more than life. I know it seems soon but the woman I am with now put me back together. I'll ask her about Maggie, but it would be a constant reminder of the past."

"I will have to go to Toronto to get her. We'll figure it out from there okay?"

"I need some time to wrap my head around this, you understand right?

But keep me posted. I'm really freaked out here. Thanks for letting me know though. I do appreciate it Chelsea."

"I know, John. It's a bit much to take in all at once, even for me. I'll call you when I get all the details sorted out."

Chelsea hung up the phone and walked over to the wall where a portrait of her sister holding Maggie hung. She looked at it every day and felt the loss in her bones. But getting sweet little Maggie back would help. She would fit in with the family and it might finally put them on the road to healing.

She emailed Diane and told her she would fly to Toronto the next week to pick up her sister's dog.

In Texas, John Porter took a deep breath and blinked back tears. He had tried desperately to save the little dog but when he saw the body of his wife floating next to the yacht he had to get to her and see if she was still alive.

It had all happened so fast.

CHAPTER FOUR

Marty waited for Diane at the Mexican restaurant they had first met at a year earlier. He had been taken with her at first sight and their friendship had grown quickly. The romance was building and since they both had serious issues with trust, they had vowed to communicate openly to ensure that they didn't unwittingly sabotage something so special. Diane had been raised for the first eight years of her life, by her single mother. Her father's identity had never been revealed. She lived in a series of foster homes after she was orphaned and had learned to deal with being pretty much alone in the world. Marty knew the score. His own mother, a back-up singer from Jamaica had revealed the identity of his Irish father to him only after the man had died. His mother battled the kind of addictions that resulted in her son ending up in the custody of Child Protective Services over and over throughout his life. He was fortunate to have finally been placed in foster care in the home of a couple who were symphony orchestra performers who had encouraged him to be a musician and recording engineer. As he waited for his girlfriend to arrive, he wondered if they finally had a chance at a normal life. Interrupting his thoughts, Diane rushed up to the table apologizing for being late as she excitedly detailed her conversation with Chelsea Stuart and what it meant for Maggie.

"It's just so wonderful! You brought her here to save her and now she will be going home to someone who will love her and perhaps give her back a sense of something familiar."

"So she fell off of a yacht, and her owner drowned? Was it ruled an accident?"

"I didn't ask that. Where are you going with this?"

"Remember I told you? I had a weird feeling when I saw that ad for Hendrix and I just had to protect him? I feel that way with Maggie. Something's off."

"Are you telling me you're psychic? I'd love you anyway."

"I'm going to order us some Sangria and quesadillas. And yes, I am psychic. When I sat at this very same table a year ago, I just knew I was going to meet a beautiful girl who would change my life by surrounding me with five hundred dogs and it happened! So there!"

They stopped in at the rescue shelter after dinner and let all of the dogs into the big playroom and let them run around and have cuddles. It was encouraging to see them interact with each other and be happy. There were adoptions pending for four of the dogs. An older beagle who had come in that day was sitting next to Macy who nuzzled him and then brought a ball over and dropped it at his feet. When the dog picked it up and played with it, Macy looked over at her rescuers as if to say, "That's how it's done."

"Macy acts like a foster mom with all the new ones when they come in. Maybe you should adopt her, and have her work here with you."

Marty suggested. "She communicates with you so easily."

"You really must be psychic. I was thinking of that option earlier. I think I'll take her home tomorrow and see how she does with the others."

"Do you ever think of how many animals we would have under one roof if we lived together?" Marty laughed.

"And you're encouraging me to take on another one?"

The couple hugged and then spent an hour playing with the dogs and patting the older ones who weren't up to running around.

"Jimmy would've loved to be a part of this. I wish…"

"Diane. You gave him the best gift of his life when you placed Powie with him. I remember when he dropped into the studio and I thought he looked years younger. I asked him what his secret was and he said it was having the best dog in the world. He's here in spirit. And he wants you to take Macy!"

"You're bad!" Diane smiled as she hugged the big Bouvier who was always at her side. "But I think you're right."

While Diane and Marty spent time at the shelter on that warm Toronto night, John Porter sat in his study in Texas and drank a martini. He was astounded to know that his former wife's little dog had survived her plunge off of the yacht they had chartered for their honeymoon. He had panicked when he saw the little dog bobbing in the waves but his attempts to save her had been thwarted when a deck hand had yelled out that Cassie was in the water too. He had last seen his wife lying on the deck, her long blonde hair flying around her in the wind. Seeing her floating face down beside the boat, he had thrown a life ring into the water as he dove off of the side. He tried to reach Maggie, but she was taken off by the current. The deck hand had appeared in the water beside him and helped to get Cassie back on board. She had a gash on her head and blood seeped down her face. She was dead. He shuddered at the thought and swallowed his drink quickly as he pushed away the memory. But it was good news about Maggie. Incredibly good!

CHAPTER FIVE

Early Wednesday morning, Diane picked Maggie up from Liz and dropped her at the Animal Hospital for a final examination to ensure she was well enough to travel to Seattle. She then drove to the rescue centre and settled in at her desk, with Macy and Harper, the beagle sleeping on her feet. She checked her emails and found the itinerary for Chelsea Stuart who was flying in on Friday to take Maggie home. Chelsea had told her that her sister's husband had moved on with his life and was not interested in taking Maggie back. She and her family were more than happy to welcome the little dog into their lives, so Maggie would be returning to her hometown after an over two year adventure. Diane liked happy endings. They had had a few situations where a microchip or information shared on the internet had reunited a dog with its family and she always felt that Jimmy Freeman had a hand in these wonderful moments. Liz would be sad to see her go, but she had hinted that Harper looked like he needed her so he would most likely become her next foster. Diane noted the flight details for Chelsea and was relieved to see that she was flying into the Island Airport that was much closer to the city centre. She would pick her up and take her to the rescue centre where Maggie would be waiting. They would then spend the next two days at a local hotel that welcomed dogs before flying back home. Diane looked forward to meeting the woman who was getting a bit of her old life back. She hated the term "closure", but maybe it worked in this scenario.

Marty was pleased that Maggie was going to be going home but he couldn't shake the feeling that some things about the whole case just didn't add up. He told himself that he had to lighten up and then sat down at his computer and entered "John Porter, Washington state."

A slew of matches came up. He wasn't good at this but he persevered. After several searches, he got an interesting hit.

"John Porter, CEO of Bullseye Trading, suddenly resigned his position due to "personal reasons" on December 16th. His resignation came as a shock to the financial community. Porter was seen as one of the most influential financial gurus in the state. He recently married Cassidy Stuart of Oak Hills."

Marty stared at the screen. Cassidy Stuart had died on her honeymoon in January, mere weeks after John Porter had left an incredibly lucrative position at one of the nation's top financial firms. His unemployment had not stopped their wedding, nor had it interfered with their lavish honeymoon on an incredibly costly yacht. It made no sense to the recording engineer who knew that this type of serious life changing situation would most likely result in a complete change in any impending plans. Marty wondered what John was doing now for income. None of it added up. How does a young bride end up dead in the water on her honeymoon with a big gash on her head? It was explained by saying that she dove in to save her dog. That wasn't out of line. He would dive in to save Hendrix, but something wasn't right and it worried him.

Chelsea was happy to pack her suitcase for the trip to Toronto to pick up little Maggie. Her girls were excitedly picking out a bed, toys and leashes and had decided that the dog would sleep in their room. When her phone rang, she was surprised to see John Porter's name on the caller I.D.

"Hi Chelsea, it's John. Do you have a minute?"

"Sure. What's up?"

"I don't want you to think I don't care about Maggie. I just don't have the best feeling because if Maggie hadn't of ended up in the water, Cassidy would still be alive. I'm still really happy she has been found and I would like to make a donation to the rescue centre in Toronto. Do you have a contact name and an address for them?"

"I understand. It's really nice of you to make a donation. I'll send you a text with the information, okay?"

"That would be great. Are they shipping her to you?"

"I am actually flying up there to get her on Friday. I'm going to meet the people who have been taking care of her and spend a couple of days there to get her used to me. She's been through a lot."

"That's wonderful! Well, you send me that text and I'll make sure that a nice donation is sent. Have a great trip. Keep in touch Chelsea."

John sat back in his chair beside his backyard pool. Staring at the water, he thought back to the day Cassidy fell off the boat. He had been checking something on his laptop when he heard the deckhand screaming for help. He got there just as the young man jumped over the side.

"Throw me the ring! She's unconscious!"

Out of the corner of his eye he saw Maggie in the water. He grabbed the life ring and dove in with it quickly tossing it to the deckhand. He swam towards Maggie, but she was being pulled away by the current. He kept swimming after her until he heard the shouts of the deckhand,

"Leave the dog! Your wife is dying!"

He looked back to where Maggie was last seen and there was nothing. He turned and swam back to the yacht, his heart pounding and his breath coming in gasps.

He helped the deckhand move Cassidy to the ladder and they hoisted her up on to the yacht. She had a large gash on her head that had bled profusely. She was not breathing. John had stood staring out at the water as he felt his life shattering.

The deckhand gave Cassidy CPR but she could not be revived. It appeared that Maggie had slipped overboard and she had jumped in to rescue her but had hit her head on the side of the boat on her way into the water.

John picked up the bottle of imported beer that he had beside him and drained it. He had a nice life in Texas. His home was modern and spacious and the backyard was an oasis that had been featured in a gardening magazine. His young, beautiful wife, a former Miss Texas, was just weeks away from delivering their son and it should all have been more than enough to make him happy. It wasn't. If things had gone differently two years ago he would've had it all. He opened another beer at his poolside bar and laughed ironically as he stared at the sign he had posted there, "When the chips are down..."

Life would go on. And now, it would only get better.

CHAPTER SIX

Marty felt like a Private Investigator as he phoned the company that owned the yacht John Porter had chartered for his honeymoon. He hadn't told Diane that he was going to look into things further because he knew he might be chasing a wild card, but his investigation into John Porter had led him to an article about the accidental drowning of Cassidy Stuart in a small Jamaican newspaper.

The owner of the yacht and his nephew, who had given Cassidy CPR, were named and he wanted to talk to them about the events of the tragic day. He thought his own links to the island would help in making a connection. After several rings, his call was answered by a man who identified himself as Damien Williams, the name of the deckhand who had tried to save Cassidy.

"Hello. I'm calling from Canada. I was hoping to speak to you about the accidental death of Cassidy Stuart who was staying on the yacht you charter out. I was in Jamaica a couple of weeks ago and I found a small dog that turned out to belong to the woman who drowned."

"You jokin' me man?"

"No. I'm serious. I found a little dog hanging around my resort, took her home to Canada where I help to run a dog rescue centre and when we scanned her, we found a microchip that connected her to Cassidy and her husband John Porter."

"That day was the worst! The lady jumped off the boat trying to get to her dog that was in the water, and she hit her head on one of the cleats. We never let passengers jump off where she did. It's too dangerous."

"I understand you were very helpful in trying to save the lady."

"If only I could have done better. She bled out in the water. Did you

53

tell her husband you have the dog? He must be so happy! He wanted to save that dog more than he wanted to save his wife if you're askin' me!"

"Well that's strange. Why would you think that?"

"Man, if your beautiful new wife fell into the water, would you swim after her, or the dog?"

"You're telling me he went after the dog? C'mon man!"

Marty kept his conversation jovial and conspiratorial to get as much off the cuff information from Damien as he could.

"He even called me after he took his dead lady home and offered me a big reward if I could find the dog's body and return it to him. I told him you're never going to find a little thing like that in the big ocean. She must have caught a current and come into shore. Kind of nice she survived anyway."

"Thank you for talking to me. Next time I come down to the island I will look you up and maybe we can go fishing?"

"That would be good man. Cheers!"

Marty hung up the phone and took a deep breath. He was on the right track about John Porter. Something was seriously wrong.

Diane called a few minutes later to tell him excitedly that her dogs had accepted Macy without hesitation and she knew that it would be okay to keep her. She would have the big Bouvier stay at the rescue centre during the day as she was so helpful with the new dogs, but she would ensure that she always knew she had a permanent home and a lot of love.

"Baby, you have the biggest heart. And now the biggest dog!" Marty laughed.

"I can't let her down. She's such a beautiful soul."

"Takes one to know one Diane."

He ended the call without telling her about talking to Damien Williams in Jamaica. It wasn't enough to convict John Porter of anything except perhaps trying to save his wife's beloved pet. But still, something did not sit right with him. He had lived by his wits for so long he couldn't ignore this type of feeling when it hit. Maggie had to be protected and he would ensure that she was.

On Friday afternoon, Diane welcomed Chelsea Stuart to Toronto by treating her to lunch at her favorite French Cafe. The women enjoyed the beautiful weather by sitting outside on the patio.

"I can't wait for you to see Maggie! She's just so sweet and she has healed up really well. It's amazing how trusting she is."

"My sister lived and breathed for that dog. I didn't think she should take her on the honeymoon but she didn't want to be away from her for a week and John was totally supportive of taking her so..."

Chelsea's eyes filled with tears.

"I know she was just trying to save her and it was a stupid decision to dive in after her, but that was Cassidy. She didn't think a lot. If she had she would never have married John."

"You didn't approve of the marriage?"

"My sister was incredibly pretty. She got by on her looks so much that life was really easy for her and she wasn't a deep thinker. When she met John, she saw this really good-looking guy, with lots of money who just kept everything perfect for her. She never challenged him and they never disagreed because he gave her everything she wanted and that kept her happy while he did his own thing. She was a trophy wife in every sense of the word. I thought she should want more."

"Sometimes what other people do doesn't make much sense. I don't have any siblings so I haven't had that experience but I know how important it is to me to be independent. I get what you're saying."

"I miss her terribly and my girls were so distraught when she died. They are eight year old twins and they are over the moon about having Maggie back."

"Let's go see her. I dropped her at Freeman's before I went to pick you up."

They drove over to the rescue centre and walked into the front hall where they were met by Macy and Chris, who was helping out at the front desk to earn her volunteer credit for high school.

"Is Maggie still in the blue room?"

Chris looked puzzled. "Maggie was picked up by the man the owner hired to transport her, about noon. He said you cleared it and he was taking her to the airport to be flown home."

"What?! I dropped Maggie here this morning to be picked up by this woman, Chelsea Stuart. She is being taken home to Seattle on Sunday!"

Chelsea grabbed Diane's arm and asked what was going on.

"A man has picked up Maggie. We have to look on the security tape. I have no idea what's happened."

When the image of the man leaving the centre with Maggie in a carrier appeared on the screen, Chelsea gasped;

"Oh no! That's John! He told me he was going to send you a donation for saving Maggie and I gave him your contact info and address! Why would he come and take her?"

Chris was in tears. " I am so sorry! He had papers from her owner. I checked her chip. The number matched. How can we get her back?"

Diane thought about it. She wasn't sure if calling the police would do any good as John actually was Maggie's rightful owner. She called Marty and gave him a quick update. He said he would be right over and to stay with Chelsea.

When Marty arrived he found Diane comforting Chelsea and Chris who were both crying.

"I should have said something but I wasn't sure. I thought there was something off about this so I called the company John chartered the yacht from two years ago. I spoke with the young man who performed CPR on Cassidy. He told me that John had contacted him after he returned to the U.S and offered a reward for the return of Maggie's body. The deckhand said he seemed more concerned with the dog than his wife."

Chelsea stared at Marty and shook her head as if trying to push a thought away.

"I thought I was crazy. When we were planning the funeral, he just didn't seem to care. It was like he was mad at Cassidy for what happened and he kept saying that he told her to keep the life jacket on Maggie but she would take it off because Maggie didn't like it. Hearing this from the deckhand, makes me wonder what the hell he was up to."

"We need to find out what time flights are leaving for Texas today. Chelsea, do you know if he prefers any particular airline?" Diane asked.

The group gathered around the computer at the front desk and before long had narrowed it down to two direct flights leaving that evening that could accommodate animals. Their plan was to intercept John at the airport, until Marty suddenly slammed his fist down on the table. He jumped to his feet and started pacing frantically around the room.

"Damn! He's after the second chip. He's not taking her to the airport. Maggie's in danger! We have to find her fast!"

Marty was angry with himself for not figuring it out sooner. That second chip should've put off more alarm bells, but he had not put it all together until both Damien and Chelsea had confirmed the extraordinary interest that Cassidy's husband had had in her dog. Hiding a chip in an animal would not be that hard to do. It was just a matter of injecting it into soft tissue. They had to find the little dog before the unthinkable happened.

CHAPTER SEVEN

John Porter couldn't believe how gullible the girl at the rescue centre had been. They really should tighten up their security measures. All he had to do now was go to his hotel, smother the dog and cut out the chip. Once he was back in Texas he would wait for the birth of his child, and then after a respectable time, divorce the beauty queen.

The perfect life awaited him. He had seized the opportunity when he was working for the top financial firm in Seattle and had found an account holding $60 million in unclaimed dividends that belonged to estates and trusts that nobody seemed to be worried about. The only thing required to claim the funds and have them transferred into a bank account was an encrypted code. There was one protected file that housed the codes. He had happened upon it when working on the top-secret files for the company owner and he had quickly downloaded the information under the guise of running an update. He could not take the chance of it ever being linked to him personally so he had taken the chip and injected into his girlfriend's dog. It was the perfect plan. Cassidy was so vacuous that she would never question why they suddenly had so much money and she would be the perfect wife to accompany him and give him credibility. If there was one thing she did well, it was schmoozing with society. And she wasn't hard on the eyes. He had agreed to take Maggie on the honeymoon if she wore a lifejacket at all times. Once they got on the yacht though, Cassidy thought it was okay to let her run around without it. The day Maggie fell into the water, Cassidy deserved to die. Stupidity needed to pay the ultimate price. She had robbed him of the ultimate lifestyle and he didn't care what happened to her.

Now as he walked down the hall to the room he had booked for the day, he felt elated. He swiped the pass card and opened the door to the suite. Maggie was whining in the carrier so he let her out. He had everything he needed, a pillow to push her little face into, and a knife to cut her open. Right now though, he was starving. He called room service and placed an order to be delivered in an hour. He would take care of the situation with the dog after he had a rest and a meal.

Maggie was curled up on the chair. He would leave her like that until...

The years spent fending for herself in Jamaica had heightened the little dog's survival instincts and now Maggie sensed something she didn't like. It was the smell of a bad human. She remembered him, the man who had repeatedly jabbed her with a big needle and had hit her as she tried to get away from him. Why was he back? She wasn't going to let him hurt her again so she pretended to sleep.

When the waiter arrived at John's room he pushed the room service cart halfway through the door and walked through to bring the platter of food over to the table. Maggie saw her opportunity and bolted. She ran down the hall and onto the elevator that opened just as she got to it. A man tried to pick her up but she snapped and growled at him so he let her run off into the lobby and from there she escaped into the street. She ran and ran. Finding herself in a park by a big old church she lay down under a bench and hid.

John Porter was livid! He screamed at the waiter that he had lost his dog because of him but refused the hotel's offer of assistance as he thought it would bring attention to him and took off on foot calling for Maggie.

CHAPTER EIGHT

There was a heavy feeling at Freeman's Best Friend's Dog Rescue and Macy paced back and forth keeping watch over the wonderful people who had taken her in. They were sad and worried and she knew that something really bad had happened. Marty had called the police and told them what they suspected about John Porter and since there was the possibility that an animal was in danger, a complaint had been registered. It wasn't enough though. Chelsea, Diane and Marty had tried to figure out where John would go before he flew back to Texas but their calls to the dog friendly hotels turned up nothing, mainly because of confidentiality. They were completely at their wits end when the phone at the front desk rang.

"Diane Daniels, Freeman's Best Friend's Dog Rescue, may I help you?"

"It's Father Tom from St. Mikes. I was walking through the garden outside the church tonight and I found a little dog hiding under a bench. She has a tag on her collar that says "I was saved by Jimmy Freeman" and it had this number. Her nametag says Maggie. Do you know her?"

Diane almost screamed, "Maggie is okay! She's at St. Mike's church with Father Tom. He found her outside. She must have gotten away from John!"

Once the second microchip was removed by the veterinarian, Maggie was reunited with Chelsea. It was instant recognition and the little dog wagged her tail in delight. The chip was sent for examination and the police determined that the information it contained belonged to the firm John Porter had resigned from just before he had married Cassidy Stuart. He was charged with employee related theft and fraud pertaining to other actions he had taken while working for the firm.

A couple of weeks later Diane received a video clip from Chelsea showing Maggie playing in a Seattle park with Avalon and Annie. She was bouncing with happiness despite the weather that required her to wear a little yellow raincoat. The two young girls took turns holding Maggie's leash and feeding the squirrels. Diane looked up,

"Another happy ending Jimmy. Thank you."

THE CHRISTMAS WINDOW

A Rescue Dog Mystery
2017 Michele Anne O'Neail ©

Dedicated to the 94-year-old writer. Promise kept.

CHAPTER ONE

As the new dog settled in, the shelter's director, Marty Cohen, phoned the woman who had made "Freeman's Best Friend Dog Rescue" a reality.

"Hi Diane. How's the flu?"

"Awful. I'm on the couch with two blankets and four dogs, waiting for you to bring home number five."

"Not sure if we're going to make it tonight. I came by to pick up Macy and found a pregnant Husky waiting by the front door. I brought her in and I think she may be going into labor, so I'm going to camp out here for the night."

"Someone just left her there?"

"Yeah. There was a note. I haven't looked at the security tape yet but I will. Macy is sitting with her. Tyler's asleep upstairs and I'll get him if I need him, but I'll just keep watch."

"The emergency clinic could come by if you need them so don't hesitate to call. I wish I was there!"

"We'll be okay. I'll call you if anything happens. I just don't feel right leaving her alone and its late so I'll let Tyler sleep as much as possible. I know he has exams this week. Good thing I was coming by to get Macy. Sky would've been out there all night in this awful storm."

"Sky?"

"Probably named for her eyes. They are just the bluest blue. Love you."

Marty went to the front desk and pulled up the security file on the computer. He ran the footage back a couple of hours until he saw the image of a young woman leading a dog up onto the front porch of the house. She hugged the animal and then stuck a note to the front door before running down the stairs and across the street. He stopped the tape and looked for identifying clues. She was petite, probably a teenager, wearing jeans, boots and a give-a-way hoodie from a local radio station that said "Spin 92" on the back. He leaned forward and looked over at the dog who was finally relaxed enough to sleep. Macy was curled up about two feet away from her. The old Bouvier was like a house mother to the new dogs who came into the rescue centre from various points of intake. They knew Macy had given birth to many puppies so he trusted her instincts.

Marty thought about the girl who had done the right thing by leaving her dog at a place that would be sure to take care of her. That took guts. He knew who she probably was, because he had been that kid. Living alone on the street you learned to get clean clothes by being one of the first fifty people to arrive at the radio station to get a new promotional T shirt. You found free food by hanging around the seasonal city-run festivals, where samples were there for the taking. He knew the score.

A whimper from Sky pulled him back to reality and Marty sat down on the floor next to the soon to be mama dog and stroked her head. She looked scared.

"It's okay Sky. Macy and I will take care of you and your babies. You're safe here."

The dog focused directly on his eyes before licking his hand as she started to pant. Even though he would have liked to let Tyler sleep, he knew he needed the help of the young university student Diane had hired to live at the shelter. It was the perfect arrangement for all of them. Tyler loved the dogs and the old house they had renovated and turned into a rescue / shelter was the perfect place for him to live while he completed his Veterinary Sciences studies. Having someone live on sight allowed Diane and Marty more freedom and peace of mind.

With a mug of coffee in one hand, Tyler felt Sky's abdomen and announced matter of factly that she was in hard labour. Marty had never witnessed any kind of birth before and felt badly that he had not realized how close the Husky was to delivering. Macy licked the dog's face from time to time and stayed close by. Sky looked at her for reassurance it seemed, so the decision was made to allow her to stay while the puppies were born. Before long, the first little pup emerged and Sky quickly took care of her baby by opening the sack and licking the puppy to stimulate breathing. Five more followed and all immediately nursed and seemed strong and healthy. Sky was tired and lay back as her abdomen contracted again. Macy stayed close by Tyler as the last puppy emerged. When he laid the tiny form down, she gently nudged his hands away and began to lick at the sack furiously to release the puppy held within. The last one born was then placed by her mother's belly where she managed to latch on and nurse. Macy then lay down about a foot away, watching carefully.

"That one's so small! Will it be okay?" Marty asked Tyler as he wiped away tears.

"Dr. Macy helped by opening the sack and that has stimulated the breathing. He or she seems like a little fighter so we will just watch carefully. If it's able to eat, that's half the battle and we can help with bottle feeding if necessary. Funny how that one looks purely Golden Retriever, while all the others look like Goberians."

"Goberians?"

"I would bet money that she is pure Siberian Husky and the daddy is a Golden. Their puppies would be called Goberians. They're very beautiful."

As Sky was completely exhausted, Marty held a bowl of water close to her to allow her to drink without having to get up.

He then hugged Tyler and sent him back to bed before calling Diane.

"We have seven babies!"

"Is Mama okay?"

"She did great and Macy delivered the last one. Didn't know she was a mid-wife!"

"Awe. That's my Macy. She's just the best."

"I'm going to crash on the couch. I'll see you in the morning okay?"

"Get some sleep. I can't wait to see the puppies!"

Marty lay down on the couch with a warm fleece blanket wrapped around him. He couldn't help but think of the girl on the video tape and the sad note she had left. She was not wearing proper clothing for the weather they were experiencing and he worried about her. He unfolded the paper he had kept in his pocket.

"Please take care of my dog and her puppies. Her name is Sky. She is all I have but she needs shelter to be safe while giving birth. I love her more than anything in this world. She will be a good mother because all she knows how to be is gentle. I can't stay with her because I can never stop running. Thank you. G."

He wondered what it meant that she could "never stop running." At least the beautiful mother dog was safe and her puppies would be warm and well fed. Since he had become involved with Freeman's Best Friend Dog Rescue Centre, he had learned that you got a lot of "at leasts" in this type of work. He was slowly getting used to it, but he wanted the best for all of the rescues.

The next morning after all of the dogs were let out in the fenced yard and then fed, Marty picked up croissants and coffee from a local bakery and drove to Diane's house by the lake. Tree branches were down and power was still out in places. He would be forever thankful for the generator that had automatically kicked in to keep the heat and lights on in the rescue centre while the storm had raged outside. He had hardly noticed the weather as the birth of the puppies had taken all of his attention. Wading through knee deep snow he saw that his sheepdog, Hendrix, was waiting in the window with Powie the Labradooodle and the two welcomed him with wagging tails and those big doggy smiles.

"You brought breakfast? That's so sweet!" Diane said in a raspy voice. " I have zero energy and all I've managed to do today is feed the zoo."

"I have lemon croissants and that coffee you like. You need to eat."

"Didn't Macy want to come with you?" Diane asked as she took a sip of the coffee. "I miss her!"

"I got her leash ready, but when I went to get her she lay down beside Sky and the puppies and wouldn't move. It was amazing watching her last night. She basically delivered the last puppy and she's helping clean the babies. I have the vet coming over later this morning."

"Is the mama dog okay? Any idea where she came from?"

"The security footage shows a girl, probably in her teens leaving her on the porch and telling her to stay after she hugs her. The note she left is sad. Sounds like the kid is in trouble and all she has is Sky, but she knew her dog needed help and she made sure she got it."

"You said before you thought she might be a street kid?"

"The signs are there. I'm going to ask around at the shelters. If she wants to see her dog and the puppies, she should be allowed to."

Marty stood looking out at the snow that had fallen for hours. Even though he had achieved success in the music business and had everything that he wanted materially in life, he was still that scared kid who had lived by his wits for years.

"I have a feeling she's not from around here. She was wearing a hoodie and yet she didn't appear cold. Sky is a sled dog. They may be from up north."

Diane could see the sadness in Marty. He was really feeling this one.

"We'll find her. And then, we'll see if we can help with whatever is keeping her on the run. Okay?"

Marty smiled.

"Okay."

CHAPTER TWO

The girl ran blindly through the blizzard unable to stop the tears that fell after she had left her dog at the shelter. The puppies were coming soon and she could not allow her dog to deliver outside in the cold. A harsh wind and freezing rain mixed with snow stung her face as she made her way through the park down by the lake. It was impossibly dark with no power in the area and she felt afraid she might freeze to death if she couldn't find somewhere to take cover. At the edge of the trees she saw the shape of a building and ran towards it. A door, half off of its hinges was banging open and shut. The urge to survive pushed her forward and she entered the dark house not knowing if anyone lived there or if she was putting herself in danger. All she knew was that it couldn't be worse than the ice biting her skin.

Pulling the door shut behind her, she shone her dollar store flashlight around. No one seemed to be there and she sighed in relief.

The home had been grand at one time, she realized, as she ran her hand over the fireplace mantle. Floral wallpaper was still evident although it was faded. She made her way to the room that must have been the kitchen to find that only a sink and some cupboards remained to define the space and she could hear mice scurrying away as she approached. Entering the hall, she climbed the stairs, their treads squeaking with age. The second floor of the home had three bedrooms and a small turret room. A heavy dresser and an old spool bed remained. She gingerly opened the top drawer and retrieved a framed photograph of five little girls dressed in white, their hair in ringlets. Someone had written in a flowery script on the bottom of the picture, "Marie, Gertie, Elizabeth, Electa and Constance, Christmas 1898". There was an intricately crocheted doily, an old perfume bottle and a button that appeared to have come off of a military uniform in the drawer and nothing else. She sat down on the bed and realized this had been a house filled with laughter and love. It was a welcoming place and she felt blessed to have found it.

Descending the staircase, the girl was captivated by a round window on the landing. It was framed by ornate carving that had once been painted white. She took her sketch pad out of her backpack and set to work. Feathers intertwined with flowers in a delicate tracery born of the ice on the cracked century old lead glass window. The shivering artist, determined to capture the intricacy of the frost pattern, clutched her charcoal pencil with frozen fingers and persevered as she lost herself in the mastery of nature's artistry. She warmed her hands with her breath, determined to capture the exquisite pattern.

She had no idea that she was inordinately talented and that one day, patrons of the arts would become lost in the reverie of her work. She only knew that to survive this frigid night, she had to stay inside the abandoned home and remain awake in case others seeking shelter were not so pure of heart. It was a lot to process for the eighteen-year-old, but she was getting by.

She had been raised by her Grandfather in an "off the grid" town so far north in British Columbia that it was above the Alaskan border. The log home they lived in was only accessible by the boats that travelled up Observatory Inlet north of Prince Rupert. It was the land of ghost towns and the brave of heart and the few people who chose to live there, respected the abundant wildlife and were protective of the land that provided for them. She had left only when her Grandfather had taken ill and the doctors in the nearest town were unable to save him. She knew the log home would always be hers, but she was unable to face returning to it without the only person she had ever loved or trusted. With a small bank account at her disposal, she had taken a job looking after sled dogs at a resort that catered to tourists looking for a winter thrill. The owner had several dogs he bred to keep his pack numbers up and to provide puppies for sale to those who inevitably fell in love with them.

It was one of those puppies that she had put her life on the line for two years ago, and now she had been forced to leave the dog behind. It tore her apart. Drawing was the only thing that would keep her sane and so she concentrated only on the task at hand. When the sketch was finished, she went to the parlor and lit three tea candles she had with her and placed them in the fireplace. At least she could have the illusion of warmth. She rested on an old couch and prayed that her dog would be safe.

CHAPTER THREE

The 22nd of December would be the busiest of days for the owner of Cafe Soliel. Residents of the snowed in city were feeling that last-minute panic and were "shopping local" in droves. Ellen was running out of the wholesome home baked muffins she was famous for before ten o'clock in the morning. She frantically balanced baking another batch while personally greeting her customers as was her special touch and the reason so many in the community looked at her cafe as a second home. A momentary lull allowing her to catch her breath and drink an espresso was interrupted by a young man leaning his head in the door to ask politely if it was okay if he tied his dog to the patio railing.

"There's so much snow out there, just bring him in. Nobody around here cares. He can lie under the table and it will be fine."

The fellow quietly entered and the dog lay down at his owner's feet.

"Thank you. That is very kind of you. Kerou says thank you too."

"Kerou?"

"Short for Jack Kerouac. I'm a writer."

"Just travelling through?" Ellen asked as she observed the backpack and guitar that had been carefully placed by the window.

"Yeah. We're going across the country. Started in Victoria about a year ago. The snow here is crazy!"

Ellen didn't wait for him to order in case the prices geared to the upscale neighborhood were too much for him and just placed a mug of coffee and a muffin in front of him.

"On the house. Ellen's holiday special."

She then asked if Kerou would enjoy some roast chicken. The dog sat up and extended a paw.

"He's ridiculously smart and very polite. I should take a cue from him. My name is Mike. It's very nice to meet you Ellen."

Before they could learn more about each other, two families rushed in brushing snow off of their coats. "Ellen! We smell muffins!"

About a half hour after they had arrived, Mike and Kerou quietly left with a smile and a wave through the window. When the rush finally ended, Ellen took a mop and cleaned the melted snow and salt from the tile floor. There was a paper on the table where the young man had been sitting and she picked it up noting that it looked like a page from a diary. The date was neatly written in the top corner of the page and it was obvious that her customer had dropped it while gathering up his things. She had noticed him writing while she served the shoppers. It felt like an intrusion to read the words but she couldn't stop herself after the first sentence. There was an exuberance in the writing that relayed events as if in real time, with all of the excitement pouring out onto the page. The writer's ability to describe his surroundings in such poetic motion was altogether captivating. As the reader, Ellen felt as if she was experiencing an almost symbiotic relationship with him. He had simply written about a walk he had taken along the lake with his dog by his side, describing the quiet of the snow and smoke wafting upwards from a chimney with such vivid accuracy that the woody aroma was clearly evident as was the post storm somnolent splash of waves on the shore. Ellen folded the paper carefully and placed it in the pocket of her apron. She hoped he would return. The hunger and desperation that had at first flashed in his eyes, had been totally eclipsed by contentment and benevolence once she had welcomed him without question or judgement. She wondered why he was travelling alone at this time of year.

Ellen sighed. The holidays could be difficult for people without close family ties and for this reason she always kept the cafe open for a few hours on Christmas Day. She had coffee and baked goods waiting for anyone who stopped by and year after year many of the same people came in to extend their best wishes and spend an hour by the Christmas tree.

It was a stressful but happy time and the challenge at present was to prepare the tea trays for the Lakeside Cottage Art Guild's annual art sale that was to be held the next day. The guild's president, Dotty Marsh had called to confirm that the usual selection of tea sandwiches and goodies would be delivered and to ensure that Ellen got her payment right away. At eighty-nine, Dotty was nothing short of efficient. Every year, she personally ensured that the cottage was ready for the visitors who came to purchase arts and crafts from local artists. The cottage had recently been put up for sale by the city and as only land developers seemed to be showing interest in the property, the arts guild feared that this show might be their last. They were hoping to use the money raised from the sale for the legal fees they were incurring in a fight to have the cottage declared a historic property that would have to be preserved. Ellen reassured Dotty that everything would be prepared to her specifications and told her she was only charging for the cost of the food. She agreed with the group of private citizens who were attempting to save the cottage from becoming yet another out of place condominium development in the lovely old neighborhood. The architecture was what gave the community its character and she would do whatever she could to help.

CHAPTER FOUR

Dotty Marsh unlocked the door of the Lakeside cottage and shivered as she entered the house. Thankfully the power was on, but since the fireplace was the only source of heat and nobody had been there in a few days, the old home was freezing. Dotty took pride in her ability to live independently and she often found she was more resourceful than those half her age. She went to the fireplace and noticed that there were a few burnt tea candles on the hearth. She pushed them aside and lit the kindling wood that fortunately burned easily. There was a lot to do to prepare for the art show that was held every year in the cottage, the Saturday before Christmas. A coffee maker and trays of food were to be delivered in about an hour. Dotty ran a broom across the floor in the main parlor and fluffed the pillows on the old velvet sofa. She was pleased that there was snow because it added to the festive atmosphere and she had always loved winter. Satisfied that all was in order, she took one last look around the room. It was then that she noticed the sketch on the mantle. A charcoal rendering of the exquisite window in the foyer captured the ethereal wonder of the cottage and its grounds in all their frozen splendor. The play of light and dark in the sketch was fascinating as precise lines gave way to shadows and smudges. Looking for a signature on the sketch she found only a simple 'G' in the bottom right corner. She turned the paper over and squinted seeing a note neatly printed on the back.

"Thank you for sheltering me during the storm. I did no harm to the property and this sketch is my thank you for the open door that saved me."

Dotty walked to the back of the house where the kitchen area was. The door was unlocked and it appeared to have been blown inward by a strong wind as although the door had been pushed closed, one hinge was broken. She wondered who the artist was and what had become of them. The sketch showed the round window, frost around the edges, and a majestic dog standing by the trees at the edge of the property. It was a mystery that she knew would captivate the arts guild. She took out the cell phone that she reluctantly carried and called Ellen at the cafe.

"Are you coming soon? I have something extraordinary to show you!"

"What are you up to over there?"

"Well, someone stayed in the cottage during the storm and they left a sketch on the mantle as a gift. It's truly marvelous! And there is only an initial for a signature, so it is quite the mystery!"

"I heard that the local news is coming by this afternoon to cover the art show so you could let them take a look."

"Oh! That is a fantastic idea! We might be able to track down the artist that way. Wouldn't it be wonderful?"

Before long the artists began arriving and setting up their displays. Dotty set up a place just inside the door where departing guests could stop and sign the petition to save the cottage. Ellen arrived with the food and a group of women busied themselves in the makeshift kitchen ensuring that coffee and tea would be available along with paper plates and napkins. They set up a couple of small card tables covered with lace table cloths to provide a place for the visitors who needed to sit for a while. People started streaming in soon after the doors were opened. The eclectic array of items for sale ranged from ceramic flower pots to large framed oil paintings of the lake and surrounding area. Much conversation centered around the fate of the cottage. Local patrons were angry that the park like setting could be paved over to provide parking for a multi-unit building.

Marty dropped by to donate a number of copies of a CD he had recently produced featuring the song "Tear Down", written by the late Jimmy Freeman, that told the sad tale of a church being torn down and replaced by a condo.

"They're tearing down God's house on the corner,
Making way for glass and chrome
I'm standing in the shadows praying
No one hears me
No one's home

Tear down, tear down
You can break it all apart
Tear down, tear down
But you can never still the heart"

He was signing the petition when the local news crew arrived to film the event and as she was aware of his familiarity with recording, Dotty grabbed his arm and asked if he would stay around while the reporters were there. He agreed and offered to make an on-camera statement about the possible fate of Lakeside Cottage. With Dotty by his side, the interview began with the reporter asking a leading question.

"We are here today at the annual Lakeside Cottage art show and sale. I have Dotty Marsh and Marty Cohen with me. Today's event just might be the last of its kind. Can you tell us why that is?"

Marty looked directly at the camera and spoke quietly.

"This Queen Anne Revival cottage has stood in this place for over 100 years. Those of us who are lucky enough to live in the neighborhood take it for granted and we see it as part of the landscape. In summer, the grounds are covered with magnificent rose bushes and flowers of all colours that we are free to stop and enjoy the beauty of. In fall, we watch the changing leaves and in winter, as we see it now, there is no place more magical. The city has put the property on the market for just over $3 million and the only offers coming in are from developers who want to tear down the cottage, pave over the gardens and put up a multi-unit residential building. The community here is willing to fight to have the property declared historic so that it cannot be torn down or changed, but we need your help. Please come down, sign our petition, make a donation if you can and perhaps purchase a unique gift from our wonderful artists. If you have never been here, you are missing out."

Dotty spoke up then, her voice quivering with excitement.

"This cottage must be saved! During the recent storm, it sheltered an artist who gifted us with this incredible sketch of the window in the foyer."

She held up the drawing and the camera zoomed in as the reporter gasped.

"Who did this? It is just beautiful! Let's get a shot of the window that has been captured in this drawing."

The cameraman focused on the ornately carved frame as Dotty spoke.

"It is such a mystery! We can only see the letter "G" as a signature in the corner. The person left this as a thank you to the cottage and the guild has decided to take bids on it to raise funds for our legal fees."

The reporter turned to the camera.

"We will post a photo of the sketch on our website and if you are interested, take a look and put in a bid. I can attest to the beauty of this artwork. It shows the view through the window and if you look closely you will see what looks like a Husky dog in the distance. It is truly exquisite. From Lakeside Cottage, I'm Evelyn King."

Marty bent over the sketch. The dog in the distance looked just like Sky. He asked Dotty if anything else had been left behind by the artist and she said that aside from the candles in the fireplace, there was nothing.

He drove back to the rescue centre with his mind racing, wondering if the artist could possibly be the girl who had left her dog the night of the blizzard. It was too much of a coincidence but he had nothing to go on. He looked in at the mother dog who lay in a soft bed nursing her puppies. The littlest one was getting supplementary bottle feelings but was doing okay. Marty felt tears sting his eyes as he thought of the person who had made this sacrifice to ensure the safety of Sky and her babies. If she was the artist who had left the sketch the night of the blizzard, where was she now? Marty called Diane on his cell phone.

"Hi beautiful. Feeling better?"

"I just saw you on the news! Tell me I'm crazy, but doesn't the dog in that sketch look an awful lot like our Sky?"

CHAPTER FIVE

On Christmas Eve, Diane was finally feeling well enough to go out. Marty picked her up and they stopped in at the rescue centre. The puppies were seven adorable, wiggly little beings that Diane could not stop petting. She stroked Sky's head and told her what a good mother she was while hugging Macy who was never more than a few feet away from her new friend. Marty suggested that they go to Ellen's cafe for lunch and Diane reluctantly agreed to leave the puppies. At the cafe, all talk turned to yesterday's art show and the sketch that had been left in the cottage. While they enjoyed their lunch, a young man came into the restaurant with his dog and sat by the window.

"Mike! Nice to see you again. And Kerou!" Ellen welcomed.

Looking up with sad eyes, Mike replied. "This is the only place I've felt okay since the other day. Could I have a coffee please?"

Ellen handed him the paper she had saved from the last time he had been there and asked if he had lost it.

"Thank you. I must've left it. I write stuff like this all the time."

"I apologize but I read it. You are an amazing writer."

Mike smiled. "I try."

Ellen brought Mike a coffee, a bowl of soup and a slice of banana cake. "You look hungry. Enjoy."

She slipped a plate under the table for the dog and walked over to the table where Marty and Diane sat.

"I don't know what his story is, but he showed up with his dog the day after the storm. Sweet kid and an amazing writer."

The cafe owner walked back behind the counter and turned on the television to see what the weather forecast was. The news was on and the reporter who had attended the Lakeside Cottage Art Show spoke excitedly.

80

"When we put this sketch up for auction on our website yesterday we were only expecting a few bids, but the response has been overwhelming! And in just the last hour, we have been informed that a gallery owner from Halifax is interested in purchasing the property for the Arts Guild to have as a studio/ gallery and to preserve the home for future generations to enjoy. This would not have happened if a mysterious artist known only as "G" had not taken shelter there during the storm and left this wonderful piece of art behind."

Mike had risen to his feet and walked over closer to the T.V.

"What's up Mike? You look upset." Ellen approached him putting a hand on his shoulder.

"My girlfriend Grace did that sketch! That's her dog Sky in the picture. We had a fight the day before the blizzard and I haven't been able to find them since! I'm so worried about them because Sky is expecting."

Marty and Diane overheard and called Mike over to their table.

"You know Sky? She's safe. She had seven puppies who look quite a bit like that dog you have with you."

"Where 's Grace! Do you know where she is?"

Marty explained that Sky had been left at the rescue centre during the blizzard and was being cared for there. He showed Mike the security tape on his cell phone and the young man confirmed that he knew the girl.

"Sit down and tell us your story okay? We need to know what's going on so we can help. The note left with Sky made it seem like her owner is running from something."

Mike took a deep breath. "It's a long story."

Diane leaned towards Mike and smiled. "We aren't in a rush. Just help us to understand."

"I met Grace a year ago when I was playing at a music festival in Saskatoon. We hit it off right away and started travelling together. Grace lived in northern B.C. with her grandfather until he passed away and then she worked for a sled dog breeder for a while until she found out that he was going to put down a puppy that had been born deaf. She took the puppy to save her life and she even taught her sign language. The problem was, she found out that the breeder accused her of stealing a dog worth $2,000 and he filed charges against her. She didn't know what to do so she took off and headed east. Everything was okay until Sky got pregnant.

Sky needed to be somewhere safe to have her babies and I told Grace we had to get help. We had a big fight and that was the last time I saw my girlfriend and her dog."

"How do you two get by? Do you have anyone in this world, any place to stay?" Diane asked.

"I have parents, but they don't have much money so I make what I can playing guitar. Grace has a small bank account from her Grandfather's estate and we go between camping in the good weather and cheap motels when it's cold. Her bank card is in my wallet though so she's out there now with nothing but a backpack that just has her art supplies and a few other things. We have to find her!"

Marty and Diane exchanged a look.

"Let's all go back to Freeman's. That's the shelter where Sky is being looked after. I think she'll feel better if she sees you. We have to think about where Grace might go. I have a feeling she may try to see if her dog is okay." Marty suggested.

Mike hugged Kerou and thanked Ellen for the food. "Come on Kerou. We're going to go see your kids!"

CHAPTER SIX

Now that Marty and Diane were aware of Sky's deafness, it was much easier to understand her behavior. They made sure that she could see them when they spoke to her so she could read their expressions. She had jumped up when she saw Mike and Kerou and it was obvious that she felt very relaxed with them around.

With Diane busy in the kitchen, Marty asked Mike to join him in the office to talk. He wanted more details about the place Grace had taken Sky from so he could investigate the situation and see if the charges were real and if Grace was truly in trouble. While Marty checked his email, a dog wandered in and sat down beside the young man.

"Hi Buddy. What's your story?"

"Oh. It's a good one. Powie was originally rescued by an old blues musician, Jimmy Freeman, and Diane took him in when Jimmy was found murdered. She knew he wouldn't have much of a chance of adoption due to his age. To make a long story short, it was the proceeds of Jimmy's estate that allowed us to open this place."

"He kind of has a golden aura. That means he thinks he's a person. Or there is the spirit of a person with him."

Marty was quiet for a moment. He had often felt Jimmy's presence around and most intensely when Powie was in the room.

"I'll play you the CD that was put out after Jimmy died. I think you might like it. But right now, I think we need to concentrate on Grace."

When Mike provided the name of the town he remembered as the place where the dog sled resort was located, a Google search instantly brought up an article about the supposed theft.

"The owner of Aurora Hills Sled Dog Resort wants a valuable puppy stolen from the premises returned immediately. The puppy may not survive without its mother at this young age and with its worth estimated at over $2,000, charges have been filed against an employee of the resort. Grace Woodland was last seen on security footage leaving the resort with the puppy in a small blue plastic carrier. Attempts to locate the young woman have been unsuccessful. An arrest warrant has been issued. Anyone with information should contact local police."

Mike leaned over Marty's shoulder and said, "Can you please scroll down? It looks like there is an update to the story. See there?"

Marty clicked on a related story.

"The Sled dog breeder and owner of Aurora Hills Resort is in damage control mode after a local veterinarian revealed he had requested that she euthanize the puppy he recently claimed had been stolen by a former employee. The puppy had been found to be totally deaf and the breeder told the veterinarian that it would be bad for his business to have a "defective" animal. The veterinarian refused to euthanize the puppy and advised that other arrangements be made. It appears that the employee who took the puppy did so to save its life. Other employees have stated that the breeder took the puppy away from its mother and left it crying in a carrier in the mud room. Security footage shows Grace Woodland leaving with the carrier. When this part of the story broke, several tour groups cancelled their reservations as they felt that inhumane practices may have been going on at the resort. The owner has dropped all charges against Miss Woodland and claims it was all a misunderstanding. The whereabouts of Grace Woodland and the dog are unknown at this time."

"This is crazy! Grace is totally innocent! This is exactly what she told me and I always knew she would never steal anything. I've been so worried that we would both get arrested but I loved her so much I took that chance. Can you understand what that's like?"

Marty laughed. "I get it kid. One week after I fell for Diane I ended up in a situation where I almost got killed. The things we do for love huh?"

Mike looked serious again. "It's Christmas Eve and I just miss her so much."

Diane came into the office then and told Marty a lady named Dotty, with an English accent had called to remind him that he had offered to drive her to church at 7:00 that evening.

"Good thing she called, I almost forgot. "Marty said sheepishly.

"New romance?" Diane teased.

"I could tell she was having a hard time getting around in the snow yesterday and when she mentioned that she always went to the early mass on Christmas Eve, I offered to drive her. She lives just a few blocks away."

"See why I love this guy?" Diane said to Mike. "He's one of the good ones."

"You can come with me if you like. I'd like you to meet Dotty and we have great news about Grace and Sky! All charges have been dropped. Come here and read these two articles. It explains it all."

Diane hugged Mike after reading about the circumstances that had led his girlfriend to take Sky. "Looks like Grace is one of the good ones too."

CHAPTER SEVEN

Dotty Marsh hurried out her front door and waved to Marty when he pulled up in front of her house in his car. Diane got out of the front passenger seat and rushed to introduce herself to the elderly woman and help her into the backseat.

"I am so pleased that you have picked me up on this very cold night! I spent the afternoon working on the journal I am writing and I had so much to add about finding the sketch at the cottage and the wonderful turn of events! Can you believe the cottage has been saved?!"

Marty and Diane provided an update as to the identity of the artist and their hopes to locate her and reunite her with her dog and the puppies.

"Would you two lovely people like to attend mass with me? We could pray for a miracle."

Marty made an excuse about tending to the dogs but Diane accepted the invitation. It had been years since she had been to church but she felt it would be uplifting and she didn't want Dotty to be alone.

As the two women entered the beautiful old Romanesque style church through the front doors that were decorated with evergreen branches, and white lights, they found a sight to behold. Candles glowed and families dressed in their holiday best sang along with the choir. Dotty squeezed Diane's hand and whispered.

"I'm so glad you came with me. It's wonderful to be able to share this experience. Let's sit close to the front so we can see everything."

Diane took one step forward and suddenly stopped. There was a girl with long dark hair sitting in the fifth pew from the back on the right side of the church. As she moved to kneel on the bench in front of her, the logo on the back of the hoodie she wore revealed "Spin 92".

"Dotty, do you see that girl with the long hair? I think that might be Grace, the artist."

"We have to block her in so she doesn't try to run! I'll go into the pew from the centre and you go up the right side. Hurry!"

Diane slid onto the polished wood bench and stole a glance at the girl. There was no question in her mind that this was Grace. The clothing matched what she had been wearing the night she left Sky at the shelter and there was a red nap sack beside her like the one Mike said she always had with her. Dotty was kneeling and she looked over with a conspiratorial expression as she motioned with her hand that Diane should kneel too. It would certainly be a more effective way to keep the girl from escaping if she tried. Diane knelt down and then turned towards the young woman.

"Grace? I just want you to know that Sky is okay. She is at the rescue shelter I run and she's fine."

The girl bolted to her feet and turned away from Diane towards Dotty. "Excuse me please! I have to get out!"

Dotty looked up and said quietly, "Please my dear. You must listen to us. You are not in any trouble."

Diane added, "Mike and Kerou are with Sky. The charges against you have been dropped. You don't have to run anymore! Please believe me. Everything is going to be okay. Just sit down and let us explain."

Grace sat down and started to cry softly. "Did Sky have the puppies? Are they okay?"

"She had seven! They're beautiful and there is one tiny one who looks just like Kerou. We know you took Sky to save her life. The police know that too now, so you are all safe. We are going to take you to see them."

"After mass girls." Dotty stated emphatically. "We must pray. We just got a Christmas miracle after all!"

When Diane and Dotty emerged from the church with Grace standing between them, Marty knew immediately that his prayers had been answered. He didn't need to belong to a parish to practice his faith. Working on Jimmy Freeman's music had taught him that.

"Going to take that stained-glass window
Hang it like some art so fine
I'll have a church right in my kitchen
And call the angel's party line..."

ABOUT THE AUTHOR

Michele Anne O'Neail lives by Lake Ontario in Toronto, Canada with three very loveable dogs. Spending time with family and collecting beach glass along the shore are things that she treasures. The idea of writing in the Cozy style was inspired by a life-long love of fiction that leaves the reader feeling reassured about the abundance of good things in the world. She began work on "The Rescue Dog Mysteries" short stories after experiencing the joy and challenges of rescuing a tiny Maltese dog named Honey-Bea. Although the dog thrived under Michele's care and eventually became a Therapy Dog, many things about her past remained unknown. The "Rescue Dog Mysteries" series follows a young woman whose friendship with an eccentric musician and his own rescue dog, leads her into unexpected circumstances. Set in the diverse neighborhoods of Canada's largest city, and often focusing on Michele's favorite place, the beach, the stories follow characters both human and animal, who will steal your heart. Michele's short stories have been enjoyed by readers around the world and the reviews are overwhelmingly positive;

"Anyone familiar with this Rescue Dog Mystery series will love this ongoing story with an evolving cast of characters that come back to life in more detail with every story. Along the way, new friends are introduced and each has a story within the story and each one has a mystery to unfold."

"Very well written and good character development for a short story. A mystery suitable for all ages. A warm Christmas story."

"This mystery creeps up on you and grows as the story pulls you into the plot with elements of survival, high finance, death and a certain piece of information hidden away. Another hit in this series and I can't wait for the next one!"

Printed in the United States
by Baker & Taylor Publisher Services